# My Tomorrow, Your Yesterday

# By Jason Ayres

Text copyright © 2015 Jason Ayres

All Rights Reserved

This is a work of fiction. Names, characters, businesses, places, events and incidents are either the products of the author's imagination or used in a fictitious manner. Any resemblance to actual persons, living or dead, or actual events is purely coincidental.

Cover art by

SelfPubBookCovers.com/Daniela

**For my parents**

# Contents

Death ............................................................................... 1
Cancer ............................................................................. 4
Fire ................................................................................ 25
Sex ................................................................................ 37
Lauren ............................................................................ 55
Horses ............................................................................ 71
Indulgence ...................................................................... 88
Work .............................................................................. 98
Sarah ............................................................................ 112
Stacey ........................................................................... 130
London .......................................................................... 147
Ibiza ............................................................................. 161
Josh .............................................................................. 177
Youth ............................................................................ 198
Birth ............................................................................. 211

# Death

**January 2025**

I awoke slowly, not knowing where I was, or even who I was. There was a dull, aching pain in my chest and I felt incredibly woozy. I didn't know it at the time, but this was from the large dosage of morphine coursing through the veins of my weak and failing body.

As I struggled to open my eyes, I heard a female voice. "He's coming round," it said. My heavy eyelids opened and I saw the light blue overall of a nurse leaning over me. Looking around me I could see at once that I was in a hospital room. The walls were pale and looked grubby, despite being scrubbed down on a regular basis. I could hear the regular beep of a machine next to me which I realised was the sound of my heartbeat. In fact, there were several machines all around me. To my right was a small bedside table upon which there was a glass vase full of fresh, red roses. A clock with a black LCD display on a light background read 10.36pm.

I tried to move but it only caused me pain. As I did so, I became aware that I had all sorts of wires and tubes sticking into me, restricting my movement.

There was tinsel draped across the window frame. The curtains were drawn with only a small gap between them: just enough for me to see that it was night-time. A cheap-looking, plastic Christmas tree stood in the far left corner of the room, its small points of white light blinking on and off, almost in time with my heartbeat from the machine. There was a large gold star sitting slightly lopsided on top.

I felt a hand holding mine, and looked up to see the face of a beautiful, young, blonde woman looking down at me. There was no disguising the sadness in her pretty blue eyes. "Happy New Year, Dad," she said.

"It won't be long now," said the nurse, an older, Hispanic-looking woman with olive skin and her hair tied up in a bun. "I'll leave you two alone."

I struggled to gather my thoughts. The blonde woman had called me Dad, so she must be my daughter, but I couldn't recall her name. I didn't even recognise her. I couldn't remember anything about anything.

I knew that I was in a hospital, and I knew that the nurse was Spanish in origin. I knew it must be the festive season. So I knew what things were, but none of the detail. It was like joining a movie halfway through where I could see what was happening but didn't know what was happening or who any of the characters were. It was all very confusing. Perhaps it was the painkilling drugs they had given me. Clearly I was very ill. Was this it, then? Was I destined to die without even any comforting thoughts and memories from my life to ease my passage out of this world?

What had the nurse said? "It won't be long now"? That didn't bode well. I struggled weakly to speak, but the words wouldn't come. There was pain in my throat. The blonde woman saw me struggling to speak and squeezed my hand tighter.

"It's OK, Dad," she said.

I gazed into her wide, blue eyes, tinged with the tears she was struggling to hold back as she spoke again. I was finding it difficult to stay awake. I had no idea what was happening and all I wanted to do was drift off to sleep. I felt my eyelids begin to droop.

"I love you, Dad," said the blonde woman. The last thing I saw was a single tear roll down her cheek and drip onto my hand, as my eyes closed for the final time.

I heard the beep-beep-beep from the machine change to one continuous long beep as darkness descended in front of me. My final thought was: this isn't so bad, it's just like going to sleep.

# Cancer

**December 2024**

I awoke with a start. The same nurse I had seen the day before was drawing back the curtains, letting shafts of bright sunlight pour into the room. Little points of dust twinkled in the sunbeams coming through the window in front of a piercingly bright blue sky beyond, unbroken except for a flock of starlings circling back and forth in the distance. The light was so bright, it hurt my eyes.

So, I wasn't dead then. That wasn't difficult to work out. I didn't feel as bad as I had the previous morning. I could still feel the dull ache in my chest, and all the wires and tubes were still there, but I felt a little more with it than I had the last time I had woken up. Was I getting better?

The nurse turned towards me and spoke: "How are you feeling this morning, Mr Scott?" she asked.

I managed to croak a reply "A little better, thank-you," struggling to remember her name. As she came towards me to plump up my pillows, I caught sight of the badge on her uniform and quickly added, "Carmen."

"That's good," she said. "Your daughter's coming in to see you later. It looks like it's going to be a lovely sunny day."

As the nurse left the room, I managed to sit up a little, which wasn't easy with all the bits attached to me, and pondered my situation. I still felt very weak, but my mind was a little clearer now. My eyesight was a little blurry, but I could see enough to make out my general surroundings. It was a private room, with its own bathroom in the corner, a flat-screen television embedded in one wall, and a cosy-looking sofa and chairs in the far left-hand corner. Pretty good by NHS standards, assuming this was an NHS hospital. There was no obvious way of knowing.

So, I knew what the NHS was, that I was in a hospital, and that I was clearly very ill. I knew my name was Mr Scott, but that was only because the nurse had addressed me as such. I had no idea what my first name was. I also knew I had a daughter, about whom I knew nothing other than what I had learnt during our brief interaction the previous day, and that was not a lot.

The nurse came back into the room and helped me to sit up. "Do you feel up to any breakfast?" she asked. "The trolley's here."

"I'll try," I replied, but I didn't feel very hungry. With her assistance I sat up and managed to take a few sips of orange juice but I didn't fancy any food. I was feeling pretty nauseous and felt sure I would bring anything up that I might try to eat.

"Would you like to watch television?" asked Carmen.

"Please," I croaked, weakly. I didn't think the TV was going to shed any more light on my situation, but it would be a distraction at least.

The nurse propped up my pillows behind me, allowing me to sit up, and flicked on the TV. It was showing the rolling news channel which was reporting on some conflict in the Middle East I knew nothing about. The country names were familiar to me, but that was all.

The screen switched to an image of London, showing a scene I instantly recognised, the familiar backdrop of Big Ben and the Houses of Parliament. I listened intently to what was being said.

"Preparations are underway in London for tonight's New Year's Eve spectacular, which promises to be the biggest and the best ever. The Mayor said that the increased sales from tickets this year meant that an additional quarter of a million pounds was being spent on the fireworks display, which he boldly claimed would be the best in the world."

Now I was starting to feel a little confused. What was wrong with my memory? I was sure that my daughter had wished me a Happy New Year the previous day, so how could today be New Year's Eve? Whatever my illness was, it was playing tricks with my mind. Perhaps I had dementia. The effort of thinking about it all was making me tired, and I lay back down on the bed.

I must have fallen asleep because the next thing I can remember is that my daughter was sitting once again by the bed. I was feeling pretty awful now, a gnawing, agonising pain eating away at the inside of my chest. The clear sky beyond the window had turned a darker shade of blue as night began to fall. The clock on the bedside table read 3.58pm.

"How are you feeling, Dad?" she asked.

I struggled to speak through the pain: "not too good, my love" was about all I could muster. I couldn't call her by her name, because I still didn't know what it was.

"Do you want me to call the nurse?" she asked.

"Please," I croaked. "I'm in pain."

She pressed a red button on the wall behind me, and Carmen returned to the room. "He's really suffering," said my daughter. "Is there anything you can do?"

"I'll have to get the doctor," replied Carmen.

While she was gone, I decided it was time to try and find out what was happening.

"Honey, I'm struggling with my memory. I can't seem to remember anything. Why am I here?" I asked, hoping that "honey" was an OK word to use.

"Oh, Dad," she said, fighting back the tears. "You're very poorly. But it's OK, don't worry, I'm here for you, I won't leave you."

"Am I going to die?" I asked.

She didn't reply, but just squeezed my hand. The pain in my chest was becoming unbearable, so it was just as well that Carmen returned with the doctor, a slim, young man with curly black hair wearing the white coat that instantly identified his profession.

The three of them consulted between them. I felt my eyelids growing heavy once again.

"Mr Scott, I'm going to increase your medication again," said the doctor. "It's important that we manage your pain as best we can at this stage."

I nodded weakly in agreement, and he adjusted a dial on the side of one of the clear plastic pouches that was suspended from one of the many pieces of equipment wired into me. Relief gradually came to me, but with it I became increasingly drowsy. I could hear my daughter whispering words of comfort to me, but she sounded very far away. Before long I drifted away into a morphine-induced slumber.

The next time I awoke, I felt a little better. The pain still lingered in my chest and I remained tired, but I didn't feel at all woozy from the additional medication that the doctor had given me. I also became aware that I was no longer attached to the machines, and managed to sit up properly this time. There was no one in the room, and in my upright position I could get a proper look around the room for the first time.

It was daylight outside and a steady drizzle was falling against leaden grey skies. I turned to the bedside cabinet upon which sat the digital clock I had seen before. It was showing not just the time, but various other bits of information, too. From this I was able to ascertain that it was 9.12am on the 30th of December 2024, and that the temperature in the room was 21.7 degrees Celsius. The figures looked blurry, but next to the clock was a blue glasses case which I opened to find a pair of expensive, designer-looking glasses, presumably mine. They must have been, because when I put them on, my vision improved considerably.

The clock must be wrong. How could it be December 30th when it had been New Year's Eve yesterday? Leaving aside the confusion over the date for the moment, I sat up and opened the top of two drawers in the cabinet. Inside I found a wallet and a mobile phone. The glasses had been mine, so it was fair to assume these were, too, even though I couldn't recall ever seeing either before. This was distinctly weird. I felt as if I was rooting through a stranger's possessions, but clearly they could only be my own. I still couldn't remember anything else about my life. Whatever was causing this amnesia, it wasn't getting any better.

I picked up the wallet. It was a light tan colour of leather, held together by a button which I popped open to look inside. There were cards stuffed into both sides of the wallet. The left-hand side had a clear plastic panel displaying a small pink card that I instinctively knew was my driving licence. As I looked at the face of the stranger on the front, I realised with a shock that I didn't even know what I looked like. Looking back at me was the picture of a middle-aged, slightly overweight man with glasses and a mop of untidy, thinning, dark hair on top.

I pulled the licence out of the sleeve and looked for more details. From this I learnt that my name was Thomas Scott and I had been born on 21st of October 1970. So that made me 54 years old, presuming the date on the clock was correct. It didn't seem like much of an age to be in hospital at death's door. What had I done to myself to get into this state?

The licence also held my address, which informed me that I lived in Oxford. I had some general concept of Oxford in my mind. I could picture it on a map and envisage the town centre, but the address meant nothing to me. It was odd that I could remember fairly generic things, but nothing personal to myself.

I flicked through the rest of the wallet, but I didn't learn a lot more about myself other than that I banked with Barclays, had a Nectar card, an Oyster card, two credit cards and about £80 in cash. I also found an intriguing picture of a woman who reminded me of my daughter, but she looked older, perhaps late-thirties. Whoever she was, I had no recollection of her.

Next I picked up the smartphone. It was a highly technological piece of kit no more than about four inches long and as slim as a credit card. It looked incredibly flimsy but was made of some incredible strong and light material. Unfortunately my attempts to find out more information got no further than the front screen which demanded a four-number PIN. I had no idea what it was. I tried 2110 and 1970, going by the date of birth on my driving licence, but neither of those was right, so I gave up and put it back in the drawer.

I felt desperate for a wee, so I decided to get out of bed and walk across to the bathroom. I felt extremely unsteady and weak on my feet, like a frail old man. When I got to the bathroom, I managed to urinate with some discomfort, and then hobbled across to the sink above which there was a large, rectangular mirror. For the second time that morning I was shocked by my appearance. I looked nothing like the man in the photograph on my driving licence. My hair was all but gone, other than a few grey wisps. My gaunt and drawn appearance looked back at me from a pair of bloodshot eyes, heavy with dark circles beneath them. To say I looked at death's door would have been an understatement.

I needed some answers and, almost on cue, a nurse came into the room. It wasn't Carmen this time, but a younger woman, blonde and to my eye, weak with illness though I was, quite attractive.

"Good morning, Thomas," she said, "it's good to see you up and about." She spoke in a gorgeous, sexy, Liverpool accent. Had I not been feeling so dismal, I could have quite fancied her, but there were well and truly no stirrings down below. I looked at her name badge, trying not to make it look as if I was ogling her quite ample breasts, and saw that her name was Amy.

"Well at least I'm not wired up to all those machines anymore," I replied.

"You never were," she said. "Well, you weren't yesterday, anyway." She had a friendly, bubbly way about her to which I instantly warmed.

This was the opportunity I had been looking for to try and shed a little more light on the situation. I headed back into the room and sat down on the bed. "Yes, well, now you come to mention it," I began, "I seem to be suffering from a bit of memory loss. I can't really remember much about why I'm here, or what's wrong with me," I said.

"That's odd," she said. "Amnesia isn't something that we normally get with cancer patients. The doctor will be round in a bit. Perhaps you should mention it to him."

When she said the C word it was as if someone had plunged a dagger right into my chest. So that was why I was here. Deep down, I had already suspected as much, but it still hit home with devastating force.

"What type of cancer is it?" I asked, full of trepidation. There was no good kind, but the answer that came back was the worst possible one it could have been.

"It's lung cancer," she said, her jovial tone becoming more serious for a moment. "I'm so sorry, you really don't remember, do you?"

So, that was that: the most fatal cancer of them all. I was pretty sure that few people survived it. What had I done to get lung cancer? Was it down to smoking? I had no idea. Perhaps I could find out more from my daughter. I really needed to find out more about her: her name would be a good start.

"Listen, Amy," I said, "can you help me out a little here? My daughter was here yesterday and I think she might be coming in again today. This is really embarrassing, and I don't want to upset her, but I can't even remember her name. Do you know it?"

"It's Stacey," replied the nurse. "You were telling me all about her yesterday."

Yesterday, I thought. Now there was a word to conjure with. When was yesterday? As far as I was concerned, I'd never seen Amy before today and it had been Carmen who had tended to me yesterday.

"Thank-you," I replied. "I will speak to the doctor about my amnesia. That's if I can remember any of this by the time he gets here," I joked. Even though I was facing death, I could still find some dark humour in my situation.

Amy offered me some breakfast and I managed to eat a little cereal with milk and sugar, and drink some orange juice. Soon after, I felt lousy, so I lay back down and thought about things. When Stacey came in, I'd talk to her and try to make some sense of my situation. I didn't have long to wait as I soon drifted off to sleep.

When I awoke she was sitting by my side. She smiled at me, her face not quite so desperately sad as it had been the last time I had seen her. Maybe she was putting a brave face on things for my sake.

"Thank-you for coming to see me," I said, hoping that didn't sound too formal. I tried to remind myself that this was my daughter, whom presumably I loved more than anyone else in the world, but it was difficult to feel emotion for someone I barely knew. I wondered where her mother was. Perhaps we were divorced.

"Dad, I'm going to be right here, every day, as long as you need me, like I promised," she replied.

"Stacey," I began, able to use her name at last, "I don't know if it's the illness, but I'm having a little trouble remembering things. Can I ask you a few questions? I know some of the answers may be a little obvious, but my mind seems to be playing tricks with me."

"Of course, Dad, ask away."

"Well, the first thing is that I seem to be losing track of the days. Can you remind me what day it is?"

"That's quite understandable," she replied. "I always lose track of the days over Christmas. It's Monday."

"So what does that make the date?" I asked. "Have we had New Year yet?"

"It's December the 30th," she replied. "Two more days to go. Remember, you promised you'd be here to see the New Year in with me – don't let me down now."

So the clock was right. How long had I been here? Could it have been a whole year? Was my memory of her wishing me a Happy New Year in this very room not a couple of days ago, but from the previous January? Surely I couldn't have been here that long, could I? My head swam with all the questions I wanted to ask her.

"So how long have I been here?" was the obvious next question for me to ask.

"I brought you in on Boxing Day, remember? You wanted to stay at home, but you were in so much pain, I didn't think I had any choice." Her face clouded over at what was clearly an unpleasant memory.

"I wasn't here last New Year, then?" I replied.

"You didn't even know you were ill this time last year. It's all happened so quickly," she sighed. "If only you had gone to the doctor sooner, but you were so stubborn about it."

The whole New Year/not New Year conundrum continued to perplex me, but I put that aside for the time being as I continued to question her about what had happened to me.

It turned out I had been ill and coughing for weeks and weeks before Stacey finally frogmarched me to visit the doctor in November. From there, the diagnosis of advanced and incurable lung cancer was swift and brutal. I was given three months to live. It seemed I hadn't even managed two months. So much for putting up a "brave fight", then: it seemed as if I'd gone down like a punch-drunk boxer.

I really needed to find out more about my life, so I decided to steer the conversation away from all the doom and gloom. "Let's talk about happier times, shall we?" I said. "I'm a little tired. Tell me some nice stories about your childhood and what you remember about me from when you were growing up." This seemed the best way to ask without letting on that I remembered nothing about it whatsoever. By asking questions in the right places, nodding and agreeing when she asked "Do you remember when…?", I managed to piece together a very flimsy framework of my life.

Stacey was my only child, and she was 25 years old. Her mother, and my wife, had died seven years ago in a car crash, so that explained her absence from the bedside. I didn't learn her name, but I did deduce that the photograph I had found earlier in my wallet must have been of her.

I had worked my whole life in the retail trade, starting in shops when I was younger and progressing to the head office of a major national chain of supermarkets. It seemed we had been pretty well off, judging by Stacey's recollections of some of our holidays abroad, which included Florida and Dubai. Stacey herself was living with a man in London who worked in the media, having left home sometime after she had finished university. She had returned home recently to care for me.

All the questions and the conversation had exhausted me, leaving my cancer stricken body crying out for rest. I wanted to find out more but, later that afternoon, I found myself once again suffering agonising pain. In front of my daughter's sorrowful gaze, I was once again placed under sedation.

Four more similar days passed, and then I awoke in unfamiliar surroundings. So this was it, then, I was back at home, as I had suspected I might be.

Over the past few days, I had watched the clock slip back a day each time, from the 29th to the 28th to the 27th. Each morning as I had awoken in the hospital I had spoken to the nurses and also to my daughter when she visited. Each time they had no recollection of what had occurred on the previous day, or at least not as I recalled it. Unless this was some enormous and elaborate practical joke that someone was playing on me, there was no denying that time was running backwards.

Being laid up in the hospital had left me with plenty of time to think. It helped to take my mind off the never-ending pain inside me, which no amount of morphine could completely take away. On the 27th I tried to get it all clear in my mind exactly what the situation was, and wrote it down on a notepad that I'd found in one of the drawers next to my hospital bed. The key points seemed to be as follows:

1) Time was running backwards for me on a day-by-day basis. If it was Friday today, then tomorrow it would be Saturday for everybody else, but Thursday for me.

2) Time ran as normal during the day itself. The exact point when I jumped back was some time during the night, but I wasn't exactly sure when.

3) Each jump back must be exactly 48 hours, otherwise I'd be living the same day over and over again.

4) I had no memory of my past life but fully understood the world around me. Stacey had a clear memory of my past, which did not seem in any way unusual to her. Everything seemed to be running normally for everybody else.

5) Based on Stacey's anecdotes about the past, I concluded that I must have already lived my life in full right up until the day I died. Now, for whatever reason, I was starting to live it over again, but backwards.

Those were the facts as far as I had managed to ascertain them, but they still left a huge number of unanswered questions. Firstly, was the past fixed? If Stacey told me I had done certain things on a certain day, was I destined to do those things again, or could I change them? I had not had a chance to test this theory out yet, but now that I was back at home, surely I could. And if I made changes, what effect would they have?

The biggest question of all was "why?" To that I had no answer, but it seemed that I was being given a second shot at life, and one that intrigued me. I needed to find out as much as I could about not only my own past life, but also everything that was happening in the wider world. As I'd already worked out, I had a basic working knowledge of how the world worked, but without the detail.

For example, I could point to a country on a map and say, "Yes, that's the USA, and they have a President, whilst we have a Prime Minister," but I wouldn't be able to tell you the name of that President or any of his predecessors. These were all things that I was going to have to find out. I vowed to read as much as I could in the newspapers and online, as well as devouring as many history books and television programmes as I could get my hands on. I had a lot to learn if I was going to make the most of this unique opportunity.

But now I had Boxing Day to get through. It was a relief to be out of the hospital, but I was grimly aware that later in the day I was going to be suffering so badly that my daughter would be taking me in. It wasn't a pleasant thought and I couldn't see any way around it. Having spent most of the past few days in various degrees of excruciating agony, I steeled myself for the worst. The only comforting thought I had was that if time continued to run backwards, then I should get progressively better as I moved back through December.

It was time to explore my home. I reflected for a moment on the peculiarity that, although this was my first day in my new home, in another way it was also my last. I sat up and looked around the room. Although the details were unfamiliar to me – the pale cream décor, the dark blue curtains and the chest of drawers, I was struck by an overwhelming sense of déjà vu.

I got up to go to the bathroom, which I instinctively knew was through the door opposite my bedroom. I paused to examine the chest of drawers as I passed. It contained various male grooming items, some family photos, a digital radio, and one or two ornaments. None of these things really told me anything new.

It was interesting that I knew my way around the house. There was a definite familiarity about my immediate surroundings. Just as with my wider knowledge of the world, I had the broad knowledge of the structure but not the detail. It was as if I'd put together all four sides of a jigsaw puzzle, but none of the pieces in the middle. I knew where the bathroom, kitchen and living room were, but as far as my memory was concerned, they were empty rooms, devoid of memories.

I still felt as rough as anything as I looked at myself in the bathroom mirror, but nowhere near as bad as I had in the hospital mirror a few days ago. It looked like I had gone downhill pretty fast between Christmas and New Year. At least my death had been mercifully swift. I really hoped that my travelling backwards through time was a permanent arrangement. I certainly wouldn't want to have to face the misery of that last week over again. I shuddered at the thought – to say it had not been pleasant would have been an understatement.

I managed to go to the toilet, wash my face and brush my teeth, but as I rinsed, a horrible, hacking cough began, leaving me bent over almost double in pain. I felt as if I was coughing up what was left of my rotten lungs, and it brought my daughter running to the room in concern. Fortunately, the attack soon passed, and with her help I was able to dress and go downstairs to enjoy what was left of the day before what seemed an unavoidable journey to the hospital. Whatever else I might have the power to change, at this stage of my life my fate was sealed.

When I awoke the next day it was a relief to wake up once again back in my own bed at home. As I had predicted, by Boxing Day evening I had found myself in the hospital, after an agonising afternoon of pain which even the ministrations of a visiting Macmillan nurse had been unable to relieve.

From the information I had gathered from Stacey, I was pretty sure that from now on things ought to get better. I had not had to stay in hospital before Christmas, and despite having been confined at home for the past month, the pain management given to me had enabled me to live a semi-normal life. The time I had at home now would give me the opportunity to plan for my future, all of which seemed destined to take place in the past.

I spent Christmas Day in the company of Stacey and her boyfriend, David. It was clear from the start that she had gone out of her way to make this day as special for me as possible. There was no denying the elephant in the room, which was that we all knew this was to be my last Christmas, but the subject was tactfully avoided.

When I woke up on Christmas morning, Stacey was sitting on the end of the bed holding a large stocking.

"Surprise!" she said, "and Merry Christmas! I thought I'd do what you always used to do for me at Christmas when I was small."

She handed me the stocking, which contained lots of little fun presents which gave a few more clues to my past life. Amongst the items were a small bottle of expensive-looking brandy, a pack of golf balls that we both knew I'd never get the chance to use, a Chocolate Orange, a satsuma, a packet of Barbecue Beef Flavour Hula Hoops, and a framed photograph of our family. It was an old photo taken on a beach, showing myself and my wife with Stacey in-between us, aged about seven, a cheeky grin on her face showing gaps where she'd lost a couple of baby teeth.

"What's with the Hula Hoops?" I asked.

"Oh, Dad, you remember, we always used to do this when I was little." She opened the packet and began to place them on her fingers.

The door opened and a smart-looking young man in a green, short-sleeve polo shirt and short-cropped dark hair came in. I assumed he must be David. He was carrying a breakfast tray adorned with tea, toast, boiled eggs and orange juice. "Breakfast's up," he said. "How are you doing today, Dad?" he asked.

Blimey, I thought, he's pretty familiar calling me "Dad." Clearly he had been around a while. He seemed pleasant enough. It was comforting to think that my daughter seemed to be in good hands, bearing in mind she was about to become an orphan.

"As well as can be expected, David," I replied.

"David's going to help me cook the turkey," said Stacey. "I've never cooked a Christmas dinner before. I know you always do it for me, Dad, but it's high time I learnt to do it myself."

"Well, OK," I said, "but I think I should be on hand to advise," wondering as I said it if my general knowledge of the world would extend to cooking a roast dinner. I hoped so: there were enough things I was going to have to learn again as it was. I wouldn't know until we got started. I began to feel quite excited about the day ahead, and come to that, my life in general. My whole past was stretching out in front of me, one giant adventure with the chapters ready to be rewritten. I couldn't believe that, forewarned with the knowledge I would surely gain of my past life, I was destined to act out my days exactly as I had done before.

For now, I decided to put all these thoughts to one side and enjoy my Christmas Day, reasonably secure in the knowledge that it would not be my last, even if Stacey and David thought that it was. I was going to be as cheerful as I possibly could: I didn't want it to be an unhappy day for them.

Stacey cooking the dinner gave me the perfect opportunity to test my level of knowledge. We had a large kitchen, big enough to accommodate a double oven and a large, rectangular wooden table in the centre. I sat at the table whilst David opened a bottle of wine "to help with the cooking", as he put it.

As Stacey asked me questions, I found I was able to answer them with no problems:

"How long should I boil these potatoes for?" she asked.

"Roughly ten minutes," I instinctively replied. "Until they are just starting to soften and go flaky on the outside, but before they start going mushy and falling apart."

"What's the best way to keep the turkey moist?" she asked. "I watched a video on YouTube where they put some bacon on top, but I need that for the pigs in blankets."

"You don't need to put bacon on the top, that's a myth started by some celebrity chef years ago," I said. "I find it doesn't help at all. The bacon goes all dry and crispy and then you can't baste the turkey properly. And that's the secret – baste it regularly, every 20 minutes or so."

As the words flowed from my mouth, I had no idea where the knowledge was coming from, but it was clear that I was in full possession of all the facts I'd learnt in my past life. I didn't know who the celebrity chef was, though. I was relieved that I knew how to do things. It would have been extremely irksome if I'd had to learn everything again from scratch.

With my help, Stacey managed to produce a most agreeable roast dinner, though, in my weakened state I could not manage to eat very much of it. David didn't make much of a contribution to the cooking, preferring to sit at the table munching his way through a tin of Quality Street and polishing off most of the bottle of wine. I even managed a small tipple myself, joking with them that it wasn't likely to kill me.

Despite the circumstances, the brave faces held up and we managed to have a fairly normal Christmas Day. Dinner was followed by watching an old Bond film on TV, and sitting around chatting and reminiscing, with Stacey doing most of the talking. As far as I was concerned, I hadn't seen the Bond film before, or at least I thought I hadn't, but had an uncanny knack of being able to predict what might be about to happen. I was going to have to get used to déjà vu: it was clearly going to follow me around everywhere I went.

I found David to be quite an entertaining young man. He was full of amusing anecdotes about things that went on in his job which got me to thinking about my own career. This was one of many things that I would need to find out more about in due course. But I was too tired to think about any of that today. By early evening I was exhausted. I'd done amazingly well, considering the advanced state of my illness.

A Macmillan nurse came in to help Stacey put me to bed, and with the help of the medication she gave me I was able to drift off to sleep a happy man for the first time in my week-long life.

# Fire

**November 2024**

The day of the doctor's appointment when I would find out what I already knew, that I had terminal cancer, had arrived.

Did I even need to go to the appointment? Over the past few weeks, as my health had improved, I had had the chance to consider my situation in great depth. Was there any point redoing things that had already been done, which were not going to make any difference? However, when Stacey rang to remind me and told me she was coming round later, I decided I'd better go through the motions. If I didn't go, she'd find out, and then she'd nag me about it for the rest of the day.

During the cold, dark November and December days, I had spent as much time as possible researching my own life history. I'd also taken the opportunity to experiment with various things to see what effects they would have.

One thing I didn't have to worry about for a while was work. It seemed I had done well enough in my career to retire with a big pay-off and a very generous pension when I was 50. That was four years in the past. The home I lived in was testimony to my comfortably well-off status. I lived in a spacious, four-bedroom house on an affluent road in-between the Banbury and Woodstock roads in North Oxford. It had a lovely, big garden out the back, largely laid to grass but with a nice patio area close to the house, and many mature bushes and fruit trees at the far end. From house to the far end, which could not even be seen from the house, it was nearly 50 yards in length. It looked immaculate even at this time of year, and I applauded myself on my green fingers, until a gardener showed up one day to do it all for me. He looked to be at least 80, but was very enthusiastic, and further conversation suggested that he had been coming to do the garden every Friday for years, and more often in the summer.

I hoped I might have a cleaner, too, but no one turned up. However, after a while I realised I didn't need one. The house seemed to get cleaner day by day without any help from me, an unexpected benefit of my backwards passage through time. Every now and then I would wake up and the place would be a filthy tip. Presumably that must have been the day I had cleaned up. So that was one thing I didn't have to worry about. Even the unpleasant stains on the toilet bowl miraculously vanished if I left them long enough.

As the weeks passed, I felt progressively better and noticed some quite startling changes in my physical appearance. For a start, I began to gain weight quite rapidly. By early November, I was looking positively tubby. I had taken to weighing myself each morning, and by the day of the doctor's appointment I was packing a hefty sixteen stone. This was quite a lot for man of my height, which I had measured at five foot nine inches and on the fringe of the obese category. I thought about going on a diet, but I quickly realised that, like many things in my life, there was no point. I could starve myself every day but it wouldn't make any difference: I couldn't change what I'd eaten in the past until I got there. Looking back at various photos of myself on social media, it was clear I had a fair few pounds to pile on yet. My middle-aged spread was a fact of life I'd have to live with. Hopefully one day I'd be young and fit again.

So, there was nothing I could do to change the past: I was destined to begin every day at the fixed point it had begun in my previous life. I established fairly early on, by sitting up all night a couple of times that the changeover point occurred at precisely 3am. The only way I knew this was by sitting with my eye on the clock. The next thing I knew I was waking up the previous day. I wasn't awake, because presumably I hadn't been awake at 3am on that day. In fact, I hardly ever was.

So the past was fixed, but what about the future? I had free will on the days I was living in, so how would changes in my actions affect the future? It was a future I was seemingly destined not to see, but I realised that anything I did could and would affect the future lives not only of myself, but also of others around me.

I didn't want to do anything rash that might affect my family, at least not to begin with, but I still needed to find out how much power I had when it came to changing the future. The only way to find out for sure was to do something that would have very clear results on the day itself.

An opportunity came up to test out my abilities in the middle of November. The local news coverage was full of reports of a major fire that had broken out the previous day at an out of town furniture store on one of the retail parks on the Oxford Ring Road. I was sufficiently well enough by this time to go out and about, so I availed myself of as many facts about the incident as I could and made plans for the next day.

It wasn't entirely clear what had started the fire, but what was quite apparent was that, had it been dealt with sooner, it would not have developed into the huge blaze that had been filling my TV screen on the following morning's news. I picked up a copy of the local paper which covered the fire in detail and discovered that the fire brigade had been called at 2.47pm, by which time the fire had already taken hold.

So, on the day of the fire, I set out at lunchtime for the retail park to get there in good time and parked up outside to get a good view of proceedings. Driving posed no problems for me at all. It was another one of those life skills that I had acquired in my past life which had stayed with me, one of many I had rediscovered over the past few weeks. During my exploration of the house I had been delighted to find a rather smart Mercedes sitting in the garage, and this was the first time I had taken it out for a spin. It felt quite exhilarating and I upped my speed more than I should have done as I whizzed around the bypass.

Then I cursed, as I saw a speed camera flash in my mirror. Seconds later I laughed. One of the advantages of living my life backwards was that I'd never see the speeding ticket arrive.

I thought about this more as I sat in the car park. Were there really no consequences to my actions? As I pondered and looked around, I noticed that there was a burger van parked on the edge of the car park. To my surprise, and also delight, I actually found myself feeling incredibly hungry. I had eaten very little in the latter stages of my illness, but now my appetite was returning. I opened the car door, bracing myself against the chilly November wind and immediately smelt the gorgeous, sizzling, fatty bacon wafting across from the van. I had to get myself some.

It was a dry, windy day, one of those where the fallen autumn leaves blow around in small circles in the breeze. I braced myself against the wind, and headed for the van.

"What can I get you, guv?" asked the proprietor, a man of similar age and shape to myself. He clearly enjoyed his food as much as I did.

I looked at the menu, crudely chalked on a blackboard on the rear wall of the van. As far as I could see, it consisted predominantly of burgers, bacon and sausages in various combinations.

"What's the monster?" I asked, looking at a £4.95 option near the bottom of the menu.

"It's four rashers of bacon and four sausages in a giant bap," replied the man. "That's my favourite, as it happens."

It shows, I thought, but I could hardly talk. I hadn't got to be the shape I was dining on lettuce. The phrase "no consequences" came into my head once more. And why shouldn't I treat myself? I'd been through a pretty horrible few weeks with the cancer. Now I was hungry and I wanted to indulge.

"Make mine a monster," I said.

I took my monster back to the car, where I sat and munched away, savouring the gorgeous flavours of bacon fat and sausage in my mouth. It felt good, and I wolfed it down in no time. Little drips of fat dropped onto the front of my jumper, but I wasn't bothered. They wouldn't be there after today. I almost fancied going to get another, but I really needed to concentrate on the task in hand.

Clearly I was no stranger to eating in the car, as I had noticed earlier when I got in. The floor beneath the passenger seat was littered with burger wrappers, fried chicken boxes and more. Every day that went by now provided me with more of these little clues about my life. The car was two years old and only had around 7,000 miles on the clock. So I didn't drive very much, but when I did, I liked to go to fast-food places. It wouldn't have taken the genius of Sherlock Holmes to work all this out, but I had trained myself to become extremely observant over the past few weeks. Every little detail that most people probably took for granted, from what brand of cereal I found in the cupboard to what deodorant I wore, provided me with more and more details about my life.

With the monster well and truly devoured, I sat back to await developments. It was now well past 2pm and everything on the park seemed to be proceeding normally. People were coming and going in and out of the furniture store and the other shops on the park, which included a DIY superstore, a large electronics store and a discount clothing store.

I had my smartphone with me, now thankfully unlocked after I had finally managed to work out that the PIN code was the numbers of Stacey's date of birth. What time should I phone the fire brigade? If I phoned too early they might turn up, think it was a hoax, and go away again. Too late, and the blaze would take hold just as it had done before. I knew the fire brigade had been called at 2.47pm, so I held off as long as I could before entering the store at 2.30pm.

I could not see any sign of a fire, but the time had come to dial 999 anyway. The lady who answered the phone insisted on taking some details from me before she'd despatch the fire engines.

I gave her my name and where I was, but I had to bullshit her about the fire. I said it was in the shop and that the flames were everywhere. For good measure, I smashed the glass on the wall to set the fire alarm off so that she could hear it on the other end of the line. A supervisor saw me do it, and immediately headed over to me to admonish me, along with two burly security guards who appeared out of nowhere. I hung up, panicked and ran, not particularly quickly as it happened. The effects of the monster, my age and all the weight I was lugging around with me meant I was no spring chicken. Maybe one day I would be, but the security guards caught up with me before I got to the door.

"Hold it right there, sir," said one of them, a big, beefy bloke who looked like he might play rugby at the weekends as he took a firm grip on my arm. "I think my manager would like to have a word with you in his office."

With the fire alarm still sounding, all around people were filing out of the doors, but these two big blokes were escorting me further into the store, not where I wanted to be with a blaze about to break out. Great, I thought. I'm going to die in the fire. So much for my clever plan.

"Get off me!" I protested, "You don't understand."

And then I noticed the smoke, pouring out from underneath the double swing-doors at the back of the store, leading out to the warehouse, I assumed. "Look!" I shouted.

Taken aback, the security guards let go and I sprinted towards the exit. Amazing what danger could do: I actually managed to put on a fair bit of speed now that my life was threatened, overweight or not. I looked back to see one of the security guards right behind me, but he wasn't the slightest bit interested in nabbing me anymore, he just wanted to get out. Meanwhile, the other one had grabbed a fire extinguisher and was playing the hero.

As I reached the doors I heard the sirens. Three fire engines had pulled up outside, and the firemen were already being deployed, rushing in with hoses at the ready. In the confusion, I slipped away to the safety of my car and watched from afar. Whilst I saw a fair amount of smoke coming out of the building, the blaze that I had seen on the television news never happened. Within an hour or so, the whole thing was contained.

I drove home, reflecting on the day's events. I knew without doubt now that I did have the power to change things. I watched the local television news that evening which did have a small piece on the fire, confirming that the fire service had been called out to the store, but had swiftly contained the blaze with no reported injuries.

So the future was not written in stone. The consequences of what I had done in preventing the fire would have long-reaching effects that I could only guess at. Before my intervention, four people had died in the fire, including an eighteen-year-old girl who had just started work there in the warehouse. Now they were alive, and ripples of change would spread outwards from their lives, affecting the whole world, not just them. The girl may well have children in the future that would never be born otherwise. They would have children of their own and so on. Potentially there might be millions of people alive in the future that would never have existed before. Each of the other victims would have had their place in the world, too. The timeline as it was originally meant to play out had been irrevocably altered.

I may have had my answer about whether or not it was possible to change things, but inevitably this led to further questions. My memories of reading the reports of the fire as it had originally occurred were untouched. Did this mean I had created two possible futures? I was aware of the butterfly effect theory, that every tiny change created new and infinite universes where all possibilities could occur. As things stood now, I was aware of one universe where four people had died, and a new universe of my own creation where they had not.

Would I create a new universe every day of my life? I sat down with a calculator and tried to work out how many days I had lived. I was 54 when I died, plus a couple of months, so I multiplied 54 by 365 and added 60 on which gave me a total of 19,770. So that was 19,770 potential different timelines I could create. Alternatively, it could be just the one. If the theory of infinite universes turned out to be nonsense, then only my most recent actions would lead to the one true path. If that was the case, then pretty much everything I did from day to day now was irrelevant, as I'd only change it all again at an earlier date.

Frustratingly, it seemed there was no way I could ever find out, destined as I was only ever to travel backwards. After much philosophising, I decided to attach my colours to the multiverse theory, as that would at least give my life some purpose. I had been gifted a power and now I needed to decide what to do with it.

I could lead a hedonistic lifestyle, living only for the day, knowing I need never face the consequence of my actions.

I could become a force for good, Oxford City's very own superhero, righting wrongs and trying to make the world a better place.

Or I could just try and live as ordinary a life as possible, but with the benefit of hindsight.

In the end, I decided to go predominantly with the third option, but with the opportunity to dip into the others as and when it suited me. If it had not been for Stacey, I probably would not have bothered, but I had a responsibility to her as a father who would invariably grow over time as she grew younger.

I had already worked out that there was nothing I could do about my weight, but a more pressing problem soon came to light which I had to work out a way to deal with.

As the days of November passed and my health improved, I began to feel a strange craving in my body. I felt nauseous and desperate for something, but I didn't know what. Then one day when I ventured out to Summertown to do some shopping, I saw a young woman standing outside a newsagent's shop lighting up a cigarette. Instantly I knew what my craving was: it was for nicotine.

The craving was all-consuming, but I managed to stop myself from smoking that day. Over the next few days the craving grew worse. I decided I'd have to speak to Stacey about it in an attempt to get to the bottom of my smoking habit. Was it something I'd had a lifelong addiction, too? I hoped not, because if it was, I'd never get away from it. It wasn't a question of simply giving up, because even if I never smoked again, I'd still wake up every morning in a body that had smoked the previous day. There was no way of getting around this. I had a choice between giving in to my cravings, and therefore sealing my future death sentence from lung cancer, or suffering cold turkey on a daily basis for years or even decades.

It was Stacey who shed more light on the situation. On the weekend of November the 10th she came up to visit and, about an hour after she arrived, she commented on the fact that I wasn't smoking. She seemed to have no idea about the lung cancer: clearly I hadn't told her yet. That was odd because I am sure she had told me it was her who had forced me to go to the doctor about it. Perhaps I had lied to her about the outcome to try and protect her. Whatever the reason, I didn't see any point in upsetting her now, so I just told her I'd decided to give up.

"I'm glad," she said. "I know it was stressful for you after Mum died, but I really wish you hadn't started smoking. I don't want to lose you, too."

That was encouraging. It seemed I hadn't smoked for the whole of my life. I knew by now that my wife had died seven years previously. Could I get through seven years without smoking? I wanted to try for Stacey's sake, but it wasn't going to be easy. At least it was only seven years. If I'd been smoking since my teens, I'd be looking at nearly 40 years.

The temptation to smoke was to get worse before it got better. On the morning of November the 3rd, the day I was due to get my test results, I discovered a half-consumed pack of cigarettes on my bedside table, complete with a classic Zippo lighter. Presumably this must have been the day that I stopped, because I'd never seen cigarettes in the house before, or the lighter. Maybe I had disposed of it in revulsion after I'd got my diagnosis. But it was there now, and so were the cigarettes, seductively looking back at me. And they were going to be there every morning from now on, tempting me.

I tried to put them out of my mind as I got dressed and prepared myself for the trip to the doctor. I already knew what was coming, but I decided to go along anyway. Perhaps he could give me some information that might be able to help in some way in the future, even if it was only advice on combatting nicotine addiction. I left the house and drove the short distance to the surgery, wanting to get this over with so I could get on with my life pre-cancer.

# Sex

**December 2023**

Today was to be an odd day. It was the anniversary of my wife's death. Stacey was coming up for the day and we were going to visit the grave.

It felt odd to be going to pay respects to someone I had never met. I had searched the deepest recesses of my mind over the past year to see if I could remember even the slightest thing about her, but had drawn a complete blank. But I knew that Stacey would be upset, and I vowed to do my best to play my part as the grieving husband and father.

As I waited for Stacey to arrive, I had time to reflect on the events of the past year. I had planned not to lead a hedonistic lifestyle, but I had had more success in some areas than others.

I was pleased with myself that I had managed to stay off the cigarettes. I still felt the cravings every morning when I awoke, but I forced myself to remember the terrible state I had ended up in at the hospital, in particular the agonising pain that had racked my wasted body in the last few days. That in itself was enough to stop me.

Instead I had indulged myself in plenty of food and drink to take my mind off it. But smoking was by no means the only thing on my mind. As my health returned, with it came my libido, which left me in a somewhat frustrating situation.

To put it in a nutshell, I wanted sex. I needed sex. And unlike most of the other things that I could have in my strange reverse world, sex was the one thing that was more, not less, difficult to come by.

For the average middle-aged divorcee it probably wasn't that easy to begin with, especially if you came equipped with balding grey hair and a pot belly. Although I scrubbed up reasonably well now that my body had returned to reasonable health, I faced the problem that the only way I was going to have any sex was if I could make it happen within the span of a single day.

I couldn't even remember the precise details of what sex was like, though I hoped that if and when it did come along I would know what to do. I'd managed to drive the car without any problem, so hopefully sex would be just as straightforward. I'm sure I'd read somewhere that sex was just like riding a bike – once you'd learnt, you never forgot. All I needed now was to find out if it was true.

Purely in the interests of research, as they say, I spent a great deal of time looking at internet porn. My hormones went through the roof as I fantasised day and night about women's bodies and the things I would like to do with them. I was like a teenager, constantly on heat, desperate to lose my virginity. It had become an all-consuming obsession and, until I could get this monkey off my back, I could barely think about anything else.

I wondered if I had any female "friends with benefits" from the past who might be able to help me out, but a search through my emails and phone messages proved fruitless. The messages on my phone only went back about a year, and were pretty uninteresting, all told. Other than a couple in the summer relating to some sort of charity golf event, the rest were mostly promotional texts from companies I had presumably bought things from in the past. Most of my emails were the same. Had my life always been this boring, or had I just let myself go? It didn't seem as if I had any sort of social life at all.

So if I was to "lose my virginity" as I saw it, it wasn't looking likely that it was going to be with anyone I knew. I wondered whether a one-night stand might be the way to go, so I headed out to explore Oxford's nightlife on a couple of occasions.

Both were dismal failures. The first time I headed out to some of the traditional old pubs in the centre of the city favoured by students. It was late spring at the time and they were packed with Oxford's finest, pretty girls in short dresses and young, smart men in the full flush of youth. No one seemed interested in talking an aging old has-been standing at the bar with a pint of bitter. I'd found myself ordering the traditional ale automatically. Presumably it was what I'd always drunk; I certainly enjoyed it, that was for sure. I ended up sinking half a dozen pints before I headed off to a kebab van on George Street for some doner meat and chips and then home.

The second time I went more for the townie pubs in the hope of meeting some more down-to-earth people, but it was hopeless. I even ventured into a nightclub but I both felt, and probably looked, ridiculous. I was at least a decade, possibly two, too old for this sort of thing.

I consoled myself that I still had it all to look forward to, went home, put on some porn and had a wank. It was sad, desperate and lonely. But what else could I do? I'm sure in any normal life I wouldn't have had any difficulty finding a girlfriend, but it was a tall order to make it happen in one day. Getting to know someone in the traditional way wasn't an option.

Out of the blue, Stacey brought up the subject of dating one Sunday when she came over for lunch.

"Dad, I worry that you're lonely," she said.

"I'm OK," I replied, even though I wasn't. "Don't worry about me."

"I don't mind if you want to get a new girlfriend, Dad. It's been over six years since Mum died. You don't have to be on your own."

I knew she meant well, but how could I explain to her that what she was proposing was impossible?

She continued by suggesting I check out some dating websites. Out of curiosity, I did just that. They varied from the reasonably respectable to those that were blatantly just for hook-ups, if they were even genuine sites. Judging by all the pop-ups on the porn sites claiming that there were loads of hot women nearby just ready to jump into bed with me, there were plenty of people out there ready to fleece inadequate men for their money.

I tried signing up to one of the more respectable ones first thing one morning, but as I'd thought would happen, I just couldn't get it all done in a day. I tried messaging various women on the site, but the response rate was slow. Even when I did get an answer the same day, my suggestion we met that very same day was always rejected. Perhaps it came across as desperate. It was very frustrating, as some of the women I did manage to get in touch with through the site seemed very genuine and friendly, but their offers to meet up the following weekend were of course useless as far as I was concerned.

It seemed that there was only one option left to me. If I wanted sex, I was going to have to go to a prostitute.

I resisted the idea at first. After all, what sort of men went to prostitutes? Bored married men? Sad, inadequate men who couldn't get sex any other way? The idea repulsed me at first, but the more I thought about it, the more it made sense. I was a special case, a man out of time with needs that could not be fulfilled any other way. Had I been living a normal life, I would have quite happily taken my time, dated, found the right woman, and settled into a monogamous relationship. But I wasn't living a normal life. Some might have thought it was disrespectful to the memory of my dead wife to go off and pay for sex. Under normal circumstances I might have agreed, but since I had no memory of her, how could I feel guilty about it?

Once I'd made the decision, I began to scour the internet to find what I was looking for. Initially I typed in "Escorts in Oxford", which directed me to a number of sites, but then I decided it might be best if I headed further afield. The phrase "don't shit on your own doorstep" came to mind. Whilst there might not be any consequences for me, the thought that in the future of this timeline Stacey might discover that her father used prostitutes was something I'd prefer to avoid. It was far less likely if I kept my sordid activities away from Oxford.

It seemed that Milton Keynes was a hotbed of paid sexual activity which was perfect for my needs. Far enough from Oxford to be discreet, near enough to get to in an hour or so. My mind was made up: I was going to do this.

There were a number of agencies, all with websites displaying galleries of their girls, mostly with their faces pixelated out, along with the prices. I decided to ring a couple to check them out. I got no answer at all from the first one I rang, but the other was answered by a friendly enough sounding girl, who introduced herself as the maid. I explained that I hadn't done anything like this before, but she did everything she could to set my mind at ease. I said I'd ring back later if I wanted to make an appointment.

The following day, I rang the agency at lunchtime and spoke to the maid again. Having introduced myself a second time, I made an appointment for 3pm. I could barely contain my excitement as I drove to Milton Keynes. I felt excited, dirty and bad all at the same time. I couldn't believe what I was about to do. But in my mind I had already justified it to myself. I had no feasible alternative.

I drove up outside the address the maid had given me, a large, anonymous brick-red apartment building no different from many others in the area surrounding the massive shopping centre. I parked up and, shaking with nervousness, rang the bell to be let in.

The maid buzzed me in and I took the lift up to the third floor and knocked on the door. She opened the door and let me in.

She looked older than I expected, possibly mid-forties, and led me through to a remarkably ordinary-looking sitting room. If you had not known this was a brothel, there was nothing to make you suspect as such. She introduced herself to me properly as "Candy" and offered me a drink. She explained that while she no longer offered services herself, she organised all of the appointments for the other girls and that there would be someone free to see me shortly.

I had mentioned on the phone that I had not done this before, so Candy said that she had chosen the perfect girl for my first time. She then asked me for the paperwork. Momentarily confused, I asked what she meant, before realising she meant payment. I handed over the £150 I had paid for the hour. She took it from me without checking it, and then asked me to wait for a couple of minutes.

She left the room, closing the door behind her. A couple of minutes later, the door opened again and in walked a very full-figured black girl, probably in her late-twenties. I recognised her from the gallery on the website as "Marie", where she had been described as a "BBW", which I later discovered stood for "Big Beautiful Woman". Not having been able to see her features clearly on the website, I was pleased to see that she had a pretty, rounded face and a clear complexion.

She certainly was very ample and I found that quite appealing, particularly her enormous breasts. She was very friendly, and led me through to a simple bedroom, spartanly furnished, with the main feature being a double bed. The curtains were drawn and there were some candles lit on the bedside table. If I was expecting the place to be a den of iniquity, full of whips and chains and other paraphernalia, I couldn't have been more mistaken.

I had asked for the "GFE" option, which stood for "girlfriend experience", and as soon as we were in the room she was all over me, kissing me and rubbing her hands across my back. I was finding it very enjoyable. I didn't feel like I was having some sordid knee trembler from some cheap tart as I had imagined. I could quite easily have believed that this really was a true girlfriend experience as she lavished me with kisses and affection. Of course, I knew it was all an act, but I was caught up in the moment, and allowed myself to pretend that it was real. If nothing else, it would be good practice for when the genuine article did come along.

When she unbuttoned her bra, letting her huge breasts swing out freely in front of her, I thought I'd died and gone to Heaven. All I wanted to do was immerse myself in this beautiful black lady and forget about everything else. I couldn't care less about how much of it was an act, or how many hundreds of other men had been inside her before me, this was my moment and I was going to enjoy it.

As I let her take the lead and seduce me, all of the pain I had suffered, the sexual frustration and the mystery and uncertainty of my life, faded away. When my release came, it felt as if a huge weight had been released from my shoulders. And it was true. It was like learning to ride a bike. I hadn't forgotten what to do.

Afterwards, Marie cuddled up to me and stroked my arm gently as we chatted a while. I had not expected it to be anything like this at all. There was still half an hour left of the appointment so she offered me a massage which soon got me going again, enabling me to perform for a second time before the hour was up.

I felt quite euphoric after I had left. So I'd had sex with a prostitute – twice. It was no big deal. I'd had an itch and I'd scratched it. I felt now that I was ready to move on with my life and face whatever came next.

Despite my enjoyment of the experience, I saw it very much as a one-off at that time, and never went back to Milton Keynes - well not for sex anyway. When I did return there years earlier, it was for the delights of Christmas shopping. As things turned out, this was not destined to be my only foray into paid sex. Many more adventures lay ahead on that front, but they would all come much later.

My trip to Milton Keynes had taken place a couple of months ago, in late-February 2024. Since then, I'd had the opportunity to see a New Year in properly, not dying in a hospital bed, and to enjoy another Christmas with Stacey and David, where this time I'd been on top form in the kitchen, roasting a magnificent beast of a turkey. It was way too big for the three of us, but we enthusiastically devoured as much of it as we could.

After a year, I had grown incredibly devoted to Stacey. It seemed she was pretty much the only family I had left. I had been an only child and my parents had long since died. She was the one bright light in my otherwise fairly aimless life, and she helped me to keep my feet on the ground. And so it was, on this freezing cold December day that she drove me the short distance to the cemetery just outside Oxford where my wife was buried. It was the first time I had been there. I had thought about going before, but wasn't entirely sure where the headstone would be: there were thousands there.

Stacey had brought fresh flowers to put on the grave, and as we walked along the narrow, stony path, she held my hand and led me to the place.

The stone was white marble with gold lettering on it. It read as follows:

*Here lies Sarah Scott, beloved wife of Thomas and mother of Stacey*

*Born 16$^{th}$ June 1978. Died 22$^{nd}$ December 2017.*

*Rest in peace.*

For the first time I really felt something. Over time, I had learnt of the circumstances surrounding Sarah's death, and knew that when the time came, I was determined to put things right. She had been killed on the night of her office Christmas party by a drunk driver who had mown her down on a zebra crossing. There had been no opportunity to say goodbye: her death had been instant.

That wasn't going to happen. I had saved four people from the fire at the furniture store. Now, when the time came, I would be there to save Sarah and I had six years to plan how I was going to do it.

**June 2023**

I was about to take part in my first-ever social event. I couldn't keep living the life of a recluse forever, and now that I was in full health, I needed to find things to do to occupy my time. With Stacey living in London, and no work commitments, I had most of my days to myself. I spent them reading, studying and learning every possible scrap of information about not only my own life, but also the history and culture of the past 50 years or so. Life would get busier for me as I got younger. The more homework I did now while things were quiet, the better I would be prepared for what was to come.

One day late in the summer when I was rummaging around the piles of junk in the garage, I came across a set of old golf clubs. They looked like they hadn't been used much recently and could do with a good clean. I took them in and opened up the bag to get a decent look at them. In the side pocket I found a half-eaten, mouldy sandwich and a half-drunk bottle of orange juice which I threw away in disgust. Goodness knows how long they had been in there. Then I started cleaning up the clubs before realising there was no point. They would only be dirty again tomorrow. I still made such mistakes occasionally.

I then remembered the emails and texts I had seen about the golf event and went to check them out.

It seemed I had been invited to some sort of charity event organised by someone called Nick. The emails very handily had both the name of the golf course and the tee times on it. I also had a few texts from Nick from some weeks beforehand. The first one read as follows:

*Hey, mate, long time no see. Just wondered if you'd be up for the charity golf do this year. Would be great to see you.*

I then looked at my reply. This was something else I was finding weird, reading my own emails and texts. It seemed I'd agreed to go before, so I decided that I may as well go with the flow and go again. It would get me out of the house for the day and give me the opportunity to meet new people.

A few days before the big day, I decided I had better go for a bit of practice just to check that I could actually do this, so I drove up to a course just outside Oxford, got a basket of 100 balls out of the machine, and took them up to the driving range. When I got there, I discovered that the sandwich, not looking quite as decomposed as the last time I had seen it, was still in there. I disposed of it and the bottle of juice once again, this time in a bin behind the driving booths.

My attempts at driving were a dismal failure. Whilst I seemed able to grip the club OK, the balls went all over the place. One went so far to the right, almost 90 degrees from where I was standing, that I heard a distinct "Oi!" shouted from a booth further along the range. Could it be that the ability to play golf was something that I had not retained from my former life? Perhaps the 'riding the bike' rule didn't apply to golf. Either that, or was I just a bit rusty? In fact, it was neither, as I was about to discover.

I had a late tee time on the Sunday, 4pm, making me part of the last group to set out. There were over 32 teams taking part in fourballs, so it was clearly a major event.

The late tee time gave me plenty of time to clean the clubs up properly. I thought I might get peckish on the way round, so I made myself a sandwich and put it in the bag along with a bottle of orange juice. As I was putting them in, I remembered finding the mouldy remains twice already, and made a mental note to myself either to finish them or to throw them away this time.

The clubhouse was packed when I got there, but I managed to fight my way through to what looked like some sort of committee table where three men, all a similar age to me, were sitting. The one on the right, a white-haired, rotund-looking bloke, spotted my approach and sarcastically remarked, "Hey, look who's here! It's Rory McIlroy!"

The man in the centre, slimmer, with glasses and a small, neatly trimmed beard, looked up, saw me and said, "Hey, Tom, glad you could make it. Don't take any notice of Steve: he's been taking the piss out of everyone."

This was Nick. I had done my homework on social media beforehand to avoid any awkward cases of mistaken identity.

"Having said that," continued Nick, "I thought it might be safest if I put you on with me and we went out last." Steve chuckled at this comment and said, "Make sure you stand well behind him when he tees off."

The schedule was running behind and it was nearly 5pm by the time we got to tee off. I was playing with Nick and two younger guys in their late-twenties. Thankfully the piss-taking Steve, to whom I had taken an instant dislike, was not with us. Apparently he had already completed his round and was now in charge of collecting the scores from the other groups as they came in, freeing Nick up so could play his round.

The first hole was a 389 yard-long par 4. Nick teed off first and hit a lovely long drive dead centre of the fairway. It must have gone about 200 yards. The two younger guys, who were smartly dressed and oozing confidence, hit similarly respectable shots. This didn't help me very much. I had been hoping that at least one of them would have fucked up to take the heat off me.

I stepped up to the tee, full of foreboding and lined up my shot. It was a disaster. The ball went off to the right at an angle of 45 degrees, straight into a thicket of bushes lining the side of the first fairway.

The two youngsters laughed. Nick was a little more sympathetic, commenting, "Not getting any better with age, then, Tom. Still it's the taking part that counts."

So that was that, then. I was officially crap. I hadn't forgotten how to swing a golf club. I had never been able to do it.

"You'd better take another tee shot," said Nick. "Just in case you can't find that one," he added.

I managed a half-decent shot the second time, hitting it roughly in the right direction, but it still came to rest in the rough on the edge of the fairway, somewhere short of where the others had hit theirs. A fruitless root around in the bushes confirmed that my first ball was gone forever, and on we trudged, up the fairway.

At the end of the first hole, Nick had managed a par 4, the youngsters had both done a bogey 5, and I recorded a 9. At least it hadn't been double figures. Unfortunately, I managed that on the very next hole which was a par 5, clocking in a pretty desperate 12.

One of the reasons I had come along was that I wanted to find out more about some other areas of my life, and I could tell from Nick's email address that he worked for the same company that I had.

The two youngsters were clearly mates and more or less kept themselves to themselves, giving me plenty of time to talk with Nick. I had become quite adept by now at steering the conversation the way I wanted it to go without revealing the huge gaps in my knowledge.

"So, what's happening at the old place these days?" I asked.

"Oh, it's pretty much the same as ever," replied Nick. "Sales targets, meetings, constant pressure. They've moved me over to dairy now to sort out the milk crisis."

"What's that all about, then?" I asked, hoping it wouldn't appear too dumb a question.

"Well, I'm sure you remember the constant price wars we used to have over milk. The chairman said that keeping the price of four pints below £1 was crucial to our long-term success. Well, we're reaping what we've sown on that front now."

"How come?" I asked. I was actually feeling genuinely interested. The world of retail was a fairly closed book to me, but since it seemed my entire career had been spent within it, now was as good a time as ever to start learning.

"Quite simply," continued Nick, "so many dairy farmers have gone out of business that there's no longer enough milk to feed the UK population. Ironic isn't it, that in this green and pleasant land, we now have to import milk from Eastern Europe just to make sure the kids have got something to put on their Coco Pops in the morning? You know, I think you did the right thing getting out when you did. I wish I could join you, but since the divorce, I've had to start all over again, especially after that stock market debacle."

I had no idea what he was referring to with either comment, and knowing nothing about the stock market, decided to ask him about his divorce.

By the time we had completed the front nine, I had a grand total of 70 on my card, compared to Nick's 43. The golf may have been proving fruitless, but Nick had been an invaluable mine of information.

I found out that we had been friends for over 25 years since we had both started work at one of Britain's leading supermarket chains. In fact, we had been such good friends that we'd been on holiday together when we were in our twenties, and Nick had been best man at my wedding to Sarah. It was clear that I needed to cultivate this friendship further, as Nick was going to be a very important person in my life as it progressed.

We were standing on the tenth tee now, a par 3, which to my horror I could see involved crossing a small lake. The others had all confidently teed off and made it across, but I lined up my shot with some trepidation. I wasn't the only one as the ducks circling around in the centre of the lake looked distinctly nervous. Perhaps they had learnt from past experience to be on the lookout for golfers like me.

They were right to be nervous. My errant tee shot went high up into the air before plopping down right in the middle of the ducks, sending them flying and quacking in all directions. When my fellow golfers had finished laughing, I had another attempt: this time it landed on the slope of the far bank, staying agonisingly still for a second or two before rolling back into the water.

Despite having started the day with a six pack of balls, I now had none left, so I borrowed one from Nick as I prepared to take my third shot, which would in fact count as my fifth. Each shot into the water had cost me a penalty stroke. Thankfully it was third time lucky and miraculously it landed on the green only about twelve feet away from the hole. It still took me an additional three putts to get it in, though.

Just as I was vowing in anger never to lift a golf club again, an amazing change of fortune came my way at the sixteenth, another par 3. Somehow I lined it all up just right and my tee shot ended up about six feet from the pin. I then holed it for a birdie. Despite all the earlier piss-taking, my fellow players were full of congratulations, with plenty of backslapping and cheering. What an incredible buzz that gave me: perhaps golf wasn't such a bad game after all.

My euphoria lasted all of three minutes. Due to winning the hole, for the first time that evening I had the honour of teeing off first for the next hole. Predictably the ball went straight into a tree, and my delusions of competence were shattered. This time it was the squirrels who scattered in all directions, more innocent victims of my golfing ineptitude.

A round of golf was supposed to take four hours, apparently, but due to all the cocking about looking for my lost balls, it was nearly a quarter to ten by the time we got to the last tee and the light was rapidly fading. In semi-darkness we hacked our way down the fairway, eventually reaching the clubhouse for a well-deserved drink just after 10pm.

I handed in my card with its dismal score of 136 on it and nine Stableford points (whatever they were) and waited for the results to be announced. Not surprisingly, our team did not win, but I was pleased to discover that I wasn't the worst player there, as they gave out an award for that. This went to a seriously fat bloke who looked more like a darts player than a golfer. He had apparently managed only one Stableford point. So I wasn't the worst golfer in the world after all. I wasn't sure if I wanted to put myself through it all again, though, and resolved to try and avoid any further involvement with the game if at all possible

After a couple of beers with Nick and the others, I headed home for a much-needed night's sleep. Just as I was drifting off I remembered that I'd left the sandwich in the golf bag. Well, it would have to stay there. I wasn't going all the way back down to the garage now.

# Lauren

**August 2022**

One of the peculiarities of my life was that things tended to appear or disappear unexpectedly. One day I would be squeezing toothpaste from a pristine new tube, the next I'd find myself rolling up the end of an old one, desperately trying to eke out enough for one last clean.

Another oddity was that I never needed to cut my nails or have a haircut. My hair got shorter, rather than longer, until one morning I'd wake up and it would be long again.

Some days there would be consequences from happenings on the previous day that I was yet to experience. The day after my birthday in October I woke up with the most agonising stomach cramps, requiring me to rush to the toilet before I shat myself. The ensuing volcanic eruption from my arse was of Vesuvian proportions, ultimately leaving me with a ring of fire that Johnny Cash would have been proud of.

Further investigation revealed that the previous evening, David and Stacey had taken me out for a meal to celebrate my birthday at a Mexican restaurant that had recently opened in town. It was too late to do anything about it now, but I still suggested we went for a Chinese instead when the previous day rolled round, and vowed to avoid all Mexican food from now on.

I still wasn't doing a lot with my days. Although all signs of the cancer were long gone, I still felt tired and demotivated a lot of the time. Attempting to form new friendships was pointless, and I didn't have a lot of energy in my 50-something body which was pretty worn out from years of drinking, smoking and unhealthy living. I consoled myself with the thought that my best years lay ahead of me, and just took things easy.

On warmer days, I walked up to Cutteslowe Park and sat in the sunshine, reading ebooks and listening to my iPod. On days when the weather was not so clement, I had taken to spending my time watching a sparkly new holographic television that adorned one side of my living room wall. That was until I came down one morning to discover it had vanished. Most people would have thought they had been burgled, but I knew otherwise. I had become used to such occurrences and realised at once when I saw the vastly inferior old 3D TV in the corner that the day I'd bought the new one had arrived. This was to become an ongoing and unwelcome feature of my life. Technology would not advance for me the way it did for others, it would regress.

In terms of mobile phones, it meant a downgrade was due approximately every couple of years. I'd already noticed that the text messages on my phone did not seem to go back any further than August 2022 which led me to conclude that that was when my upgrade must have taken place. Finding the instruction booklet for my phone, I discovered that it ought to have been a relatively simple task to port my old messages over to the new phone but, for whatever reason, I hadn't done so.

So it came as no surprise to me one morning in August when I woke up to discover an older, slightly battle-scarred phone sitting on my bedside table. I'd never seen it before, so presumably I must have got rid of it as soon as I'd got the new one.

Eager to see what secrets this older phone might be hiding, I switched it on to be confronted by the familiar PIN code unlock screen. Hoping that I'd had the sense to use the same PIN as on the other phone, I tried it, and thankfully it worked. I'd had no end of trouble with PIN codes and passwords already over the past couple of years, so it was a relief not to have to go through all of that again. I'd only recently begun to be able to use the cashpoint. A thorough search through some piles of untidy receipts in an old briefcase had revealed a small scrap of paper with my PIN number written on it. It also said, "Please memorise and destroy this strip" beneath it. It was a good job I hadn't.

This phone was packed with far more information than the other one had been. My contacts list had expanded dramatically, and the text messages now went back years. Excited at this fresh new source of information, I quickly began to scroll through them.

A few pages up from all of the usual crap was a message that stood out like a sore thumb: it was from someone called Lauren. I could only see the first few words which read *Hey, you, sorry I've not been in touch for a couple of days, but...*

Eagerly I clicked on it to read the full message:

*Hey, you, sorry I've not been in touch for a couple of days, but I've kind of met someone else. Thanks for everything, it's been fun, Lauren xx*

This was the last in a string of messages, but it was the one just above it, sent three days previously which really got me excited:

*I am gonna totally fuck your brains out tonight.*

I scrolled through the messages. There were dozens of them, all sent over a brief period of a few days in January. My own replies were there, too, and I was quite shocked at the filth I had written back in response.

And it wasn't just text messages. She had sent me several pictures of herself, from her pretty cheeky face to intimate shots of her private parts. I felt myself getting incredibly turned on as I looked at the pictures and also a little bit like a dirty old man. This girl couldn't have been any older than Stacey. How on earth had I managed to pull her?

I wasn't going to worry about that. I was well and truly on a promise and if a girl in her twenties wanted to give herself on a plate to a man my age, who was I to question it? There was nothing illegal about it.

I needed to relieve my excitement but I also desperately needed the toilet, so I headed for the bathroom first. So engrossed was I in reading her messages, that I carried on as I went for a wee, unzipping my flies with my right hand while I carried on reading, holding the phone in my left. Unfortunately in my growing state of excitement I completely failed to take aim correctly and in my haste to correct the problem lost my grip on the phone which fell straight into the toilet.

To say this put a dampener on my excitement would have been an understatement, particularly when I fished the phone out to discover it no longer worked. Good job I was getting a new one, really. In fact, maybe that was why I'd got a new one: had something similar happened in my previous timeline? It would certainly explain the lack of contacts and messages on the new phone.

Annoyed at having lost the phone just as I'd discovered that I was about to embark on a sexual adventure with a hot, young girl, I tried to put it out of my mind for the rest of the day, but I couldn't. My one experience with the escort in Milton Keynes seemed an awful long time ago now, and the fact that someone now wanted to have consensual sex with me with no money changing hands was thrilling. It certainly put a spring in my step as I headed up to the park. At last I had something to look forward to in the near future.

Thankfully, the phone was back on my bedside table when I awoke the following morning, which enabled me to analyse Lauren's messages in more detail. They spanned a grand total of six days in January, so it seemed whatever we'd had, it hadn't lasted long.

January was still seven months away, which was a tantalisingly long time to wait. I wondered if there was anything I could do to speed things up, and after careful consideration, I decided to test the waters with a text message.

*Hi, Lauren, long time no see. Just wondered if you fancied meeting up for a drink some time x*

The response to this message was a resounding silence. I sent it at 6pm, but no reply came that day. I suppose she could have not replied until the next day, in which case it would have been too late for me to have seen it, but I doubted it. Most people responded to text messages pretty quickly. I had to resign myself to the fact that she didn't want to see me, and that was that. Never mind, she'd be all over me like a rash come January, so I'd just bide my time and wait for my Christmas to come early.

Her last message had been sent on the 11th of January, her first on the 6th. The one about "fucking my brains out" had been sent on the 9th which was a Sunday, according to my diary.

Most people didn't look forward to early January but I couldn't wait for it to come round.


**January 2022**

Most Sundays, Stacey came up from London to visit, sometimes bringing David, sometimes not. When she visited on the 16th of January, she mentioned that she'd missed me the previous Sunday and enquired as to whether or not I'd enjoyed my golf. Clearly I must have told her that that was what I had been doing, so I made a mental note to ring her early on Sunday morning to tell her. Quite why anyone in their right mind would want to go out and play golf on a freezing cold day in January was beyond me. I had a much more enjoyable game in mind, and it wasn't golf balls that were going to be getting a workout.

On the 10th of January, for the first time since I had left hospital, I awoke to find myself somewhere other than at home in my own bed. It was daylight outside and there was just enough sunshine coming in through the gap in the curtains for me to make out my surroundings. I was in a bedroom much smaller than my own, with barely enough room to house the double bed I was in. The walls had been painted white, quite some time ago by the look of them, as the paint was peeling off everywhere. A few posters of bands I had never heard of adorned the walls. The room was sorely in need of some redecoration.

All of that took but a split second to take in. Of far greater interest was the gorgeous-looking creature curled up next to me in the bed. She was fast asleep, facing me and snoring softly.

She was just as I had seen her in the pictures on my phone. She had quite a chubby face, fringed by a sharply cut bob of dark hair which complemented her face perfectly. Instinctively I reached across and cuddled up to her. She seemed much more petite than I had imagined, her feet seeming barely to go down much below my knee, but to be fair, she was quite curled up.

I kissed her and she awoke, smiling. "Morning, gorgeous," she said. She had an infectious, cheeky grin and I couldn't keep my hands off her, running them along her body, wanting more.

"Mmmm, you're frisky this morning," she remarked. "Didn't you have enough last night?" And with that, she pushed me over onto my back and wriggled her way down the bed. I really hoped she might be about to do what I thought she was about to do, and I wasn't disappointed.

The next ten minutes were a blur of ecstasy. Afterwards, Lauren reached across to a tiny bedside table, took a cigarette out from a packet, and lit up. "Want one?" she asked.

"No – I don't smoke," I said, though I was sorely tempted. I'd learnt to manage my nicotine cravings, but having this cute, sexy girl, who had just done what she had done, coolly lighting up next to me was extremely tempting.

"You could have fooled me," she said. "You were chaining them last night."

I realise I'd made a slip and quickly said, "Yes, I know, but I'm supposed to be giving up, New Year's resolution and all that."

She looked across to the clock, which read 9.12am. "I'm going to have to get moving, I'm due in work at ten."

"What do you do?" I asked, and then quickly realised I'd made another mistake. She looked annoyed as she replied, "I told you all about that yesterday, obviously you weren't listening. I'm working as a beautician in a salon in town."

"Will I see you later?" I asked, hopefully, slightly disappointed that our morning together was going to be cut short so soon.

"I can't tonight. I'm going out with my friend, Kaylee. I'll text you tomorrow, yeah?"

"OK," I said. I had no reason to be bothered. I already knew she was going to dump me the next day, and I had all the pleasures of the previous days still to come.

We left at the same time, emerging out into a busy Walton Street, the low winter sun making me squint. We kissed goodbye and she headed into town, whilst I began the two-mile walk home back to North Oxford. It was cold and frosty, but I was still well and truly basking in the afterglow.

I wasn't surprised when I didn't hear from Lauren again that day. I already knew that there would be no text messages, and she didn't call. I pondered over what she'd said and the text that had come the day after. The most obvious explanation was that she'd gone out with her friend, met another bloke, and decided to drop me for him. I didn't feel particularly bitter: after all, I'd been punching well above my weight to have got with her in the first place.

The next day was Sunday, and I did not wake up in Lauren's bedsit, but back home in my own bed. I checked my phone. The message about fucking my brains out had disappeared. How was I going to play this? I should have asked her what we'd done the previous day when I had the chance, but I had been rather distracted on the Monday morning and then she'd rushed off to work.

I remembered that she'd sent the message just before midday, so I waited until about a quarter to twelve, and then rang her.

She sounded genuinely pleased to hear me and full of enthusiasm when I asked her if she fancied meeting up for Sunday lunch. There was a lot of flirty talk on the phone, and sure enough the famous "brains" text arrived shortly afterwards, word for word exactly as it had done before. I was in for a good day.

I met her in a riverside pub by the Thames, which I had heard did a fantastic Sunday roast. I wasn't disappointed. Over a huge helping of roast beef, Yorkshire pudding and all the trimmings, I asked her more about herself, choosing my words carefully, being mindful of the mistake I had made before.

I found out that she was nineteen years old, younger than I had originally thought, and had been living in Oxford for about a year. She had moved to be with her boyfriend who was an undergraduate at the university, but they had split up a few months ago.

Now she was eking out a living working as a beautician at a salon, but was struggling to make ends meet. Although she only had a rented room in a shared house, rents in Oxford were prohibitively expensive and she was considering moving back to her home town, around fifteen miles away, to live with her mother.

Between us we downed two bottles of wine over lunch, by which time Lauren was very much ready to act out her promise from the text message. Months of anticipation were welling up inside me as we took a taxi back to her bedsit. Once we were there, I wasn't disappointed, and thankfully, I'm pleased to say, neither was she. Despite my age and relative lack of fitness, it seemed I'd still got it. Maybe it was a little sick, a 51-year-old man having sex with a nineteen-year-old, but realistically, how many men of my age would turn down such an offer?

After a couple of amazing hours in the sack, she lit up and flicked on the TV, a fairly small and old-fashioned flat-screen model which sat atop her chest of drawers.

"Oh, I love this movie," she exclaimed. "Let's watch."

It was one of the old *Back to the Future* movies of which I was vaguely aware, but hadn't seen before, at least not in this lifetime. We snuggled up together under the duvet and watched as the lead character jumped back and forth between 1955, 1985 and 2015.

"Wouldn't it be great if people really could travel in time?" I commented, fully aware of the ironic nature of my statement.

"Oh, they can," replied Lauren casually, taking me by surprise. "I should know. I've seen it."

"Really?" I asked, intrigued. "Tell me more," I said.

"I shouldn't, to be honest," she said. "I made a promise with a group of friends that we'd never talk about it to anyone else."

"You can't say something like that and then not elaborate on it," I said. And then I added: "You know, I may well know more about time travel than you might suspect. What if I told you that I'd travelled in time myself?"

"I'd probably think you were making it up," she said.

For all I knew, she might be making it up as well. But there was no harm in finding out.

"OK, how about this, then?" I said. "Whether we're making it up or not, why don't you tell me your story, and I'll tell you mine. If it's all one big fantasy, then what harm can it do?"

"Sounds good to me," said Lauren. "I like fantasies."

"I bet you do," I said. "Come on then, you first."

And so Lauren told me the tale of how she and her friends had discovered a Time Bubble in a railway tunnel and how they had used it to jump forward in time. Although she hadn't personally travelled through it herself, she'd watched as her friend, who'd mysteriously vanished for two days, reappeared before her very eyes. She said she had to keep some of the details secret, such as the time and location where all this had happened. This was for the protection of someone who was currently travelling inside the Time

Bubble. Lack of details notwithstanding, it certainly was an interesting tale.

If it was true, it meant that I was no longer alone in the time-travelling world. Up until now, I had not told anyone about my own situation, firstly because there did not seem a lot of point when they would not remember it the next day, and secondly because I just assumed anyone I told would assume I was mad.

So I decided that I would tell Lauren everything. Right from the first day when I'd woken up in the hospital bed, all the way back to today, including the fact that I had known for several months that we were destined to meet as we had done.

She listened intently all the way through, asking occasional questions for clarification. When I had finished I asked her what she thought.

"Well," she replied, "had you told me all this three years ago, I would have said you were insane. But after what I've seen since then, I guess anything is possible."

"I wish there was a way I could prove it to you," I responded, "but unfortunately one of the drawbacks of my journey backward through time is I can't bring anything with me. Otherwise, I could have given you a copy of tomorrow's paper."

"That's convenient," she said, and then added, "I'm only joking – I really would like to believe you."

Then I remembered something. "OK, there is a way I can prove it. Unfortunately you won't find out today so it won't be any good to me, but at least you will know I was telling the truth when it happens."

"Go on," she said.

"Right, it's quite simple really. Oxford United are going to win 4-0 this Saturday," I said.

"Now I know you're making it up!" she said, laughing. "When was the last time Oxford managed to win 4-0?"

"I know, and that's what makes it all the more likely I'm telling the truth when it happens." Oxford were currently just above the relegation zone in their division, with little sign of any improvement to come.

"If you know the results of football matches, you should bet on them," remarked Lauren.

"I thought about it once," I said, "but then I realised it was pointless as any money I won would be gone the next day. However, now you've mentioned it, I might sometime, just for the thrill of it. But I am telling you now, Oxford are going to win 4-0 this Saturday."

"What are the odds on that?" asked Lauren. "Must be pretty good, don't you think?"

I didn't know very much about gambling, so couldn't really answer her question, but 4-0 seemed a quite unlikely scoreline, especially where Oxford were concerned. "I've no idea," I said, "but they've got to be good. I really think you should put a bet on it. You said yourself you were struggling to afford the rent on this place. I think you should go down to the betting shop and put every penny you can on Oxford winning 4-0. It could make the difference between you staying in Oxford or having to move back home."

"OK, you've convinced me," she said. "I've got about a month left here at best with the money I've got, so what is there to lose?"

"Nothing," I said. "In fact, I'm so confident I am going to give you the money myself," and I reached down to my trousers which had been discarded in a heap next to the bed in our rush to get into bed, and pulled out two £20 pound notes. "Take these, and promise me you'll put the bet on."

"Ooh, I'm excited now," said Lauren. "Don't you think this is a bit dodgy, though, you handing me over cash after what we did earlier? I'm not that kind of girl, you know." She laughed again, her eyes flashing me another one of her naughty looks that I was getting to know so well. I was becoming really fond of this girl, and was going to miss her when our short time was over.

"Well, since you are helping me out," she said, "maybe I can do something for you, too."

"What's that?" I asked, my mind immediately imagining a further feast of sexual delights.

"I think you should go and speak to my ex, Josh. He has been obsessed with time travel ever since he discovered it was possible. Since he's been at the university, he's been getting involved with some time travel experiments they are doing there."

Now this was very interesting. I had assumed my journey was one-way only, always going backwards, never being able to see the results of my actions on future events. What if it was possible to change that?

"I think I'd like to meet him," I said.

"I'll give you his number," she said, and wrote it down on a piece of paper. I took it, but before I could memorise it, she pounced on me once again and all thoughts of time travel were very quickly forgotten.

The following morning, I again awoke in her bed, cuddled up to her. I reached across to the bedside table for the note she had written, but of course, it was gone. I really had to stop making that mistake.

"Hey, sexy," I breathed in her ear as I gently woke her. She turned and smiled and we kissed. It was Saturday and she had to work, so there was little time to talk. I needed to get Josh's number from her again, but since all memory of the conversation we'd had would now have been erased from her mind, I couldn't just come out and ask her. It wasn't urgent. The fact that I'd woken up in her bed on Saturday morning meant that I'd be seeing her on Friday night, so I'd find a way of getting it out of her then.

Unfortunately, she didn't seem anything like as receptive to talking about her ex on Friday night, perhaps because she'd only known me a day or two at that stage. She seemed mainly interested in getting pissed and having a good time. With some reluctance I allowed myself to be dragged along to a club, bearing in mind my only previous visit as a sad, single, middle-aged man had been a dismal failure. This time was different. With a sexy young girl in tow I no longer felt like a loser and even managed a few steps on the dance floor, amazed at my bravery. For a while I forgot my age, and found myself really enjoying myself in public for possibly the first time ever.

Unfortunately, I was about to have my very own Cinderella moment. I had stayed up until 3am before, but always in the safety of my own home. I had been having such a good night that I had lost all track of time. Lauren and I had left the dance floor to get some more drinks and move to a quieter area of the club. Here there were small, circular recesses set into the walls like bay windows, with a small circular bench just big enough for a couple to sit in.

We were sitting in one of these cubicles when suddenly the world around me vanished and I found myself at home, on the toilet, having a sitting down wee. To say this put a bit of a dampener on proceedings would have been putting it mildly.

Usually when my 3am jump back in time occurred I was asleep either at the time I left the future, or at the time I returned to the past. I couldn't recall another occasion when I had been awake for both. It got me wondering what had happened to my future self in the club. Was I still in the booth, after 3am, kissing Lauren, and if I was, would I still be me, or would I be another me, starting another timeline? There was still no way of knowing these things. All I knew now was that my best lead so far towards answering these questions was to find Josh.

# Horses

**December 2021**

I had only one day left with Lauren after my Cinderella exit from the club, and that was the day when I first met her. It was quite a bittersweet moment for me, knowing that I wouldn't see her anymore.

I knew where and when we'd initially met from our conversations, and so it was that I made sure I was in the coffee shop at the appointed time. I needed to engineer things to ensure that our chance meeting took place on cue.

Apparently I had bumped into her and knocked her coffee out of her hand at which point I'd offered to buy her another. In the original timeline, it was no doubt a simple accident. My attempt to re-enact the scenario this time round must have looked like a blatantly contrived effort, but it still did the trick. It got us talking and we had a very enjoyable day together which ended with us arranging to meet again the following day.

Now that our little fling was over, I pondered what it was she'd seen in me. Perhaps I was something different, a father figure perhaps? I guess I would never know now. I decided just to be grateful for whatever good fortune had brought her into my life for all too brief a time, and move on alone once more.

Her departure from my life was something I realised I was going to have to get used to with other people in the future. Just as my tomorrows would be everybody else's yesterdays, I'd be saying goodbye to people for the last time while they were meeting me for the first time.

I hadn't needed to ask Lauren any more about Josh, as I'd already found out everything I needed to know from social media. Having checked out her profile on Facebook, I was pleased to discover that it was open to public view for all and sundry to browse, friends or not. And she certainly had a lot of friends, as well as followers: mostly male, it seemed.

It was a relatively simple task to find Josh on Lauren's Friends list. Before long I knew that his name was Josh Gardner; he was twenty years old and a second-year undergraduate at one of Oxford's most prestigious colleges. I also knew from his profile picture exactly what he looked like. All I needed to do now was to work out how to meet him.

By the time I had done this detective work it had been early January, and he had gone back to his home town for the Christmas period. So I decided to wait until mid-December when he would be back at college and then try to work out a way to approach him.

Social media again proved very useful for this purpose. Just as with email, text messaging and Wikipedia, Facebook was a rich source of information to help guide me through my life. Josh also had an open profile, and by reading back through his status messages I could establish a number of places and times where he would be. I just needed to pick the right moment. I also needed a good "convincer". This was a term I had seen on TV in a programme about confidence tricksters. I was no conman, but I knew if I was to ensure that Josh was to believe my story, I'd have to find some way of backing it up.

As luck would have it, a scroll back through Josh's profile revealed the perfect opportunity. It seemed that one Saturday in early December he had gone to the races at Cheltenham with his dad and brother. So, I wouldn't need to contrive a way of meeting in Oxford after all. It looked like I was about to pay my first of many visits to the racetrack.

I had a vague interest in racing from watching it on Channel 4, mostly during that first year or so when I hadn't felt up to leaving the house very often. I got quite a kick out of knowing the results in advance, particularly when I heard the channel's experts confidently predicting that such and such a horse (usually the favourite) would win when I knew otherwise.

However, there didn't seem to me to be much point in betting on it. As I'd explained to Lauren, my winnings would be destined to vanish as soon as the day was out, so why bother?

But on this occasion my goal was not to win money. It was to convince Josh that I knew the future and the race meeting was the perfect place. Once I'd tipped him a few winners, I could broach the idea of time travel with him and see what the response was. If there was any possibility that he could shed any further light on my situation, I had to find out. Of course there was every chance that this would all turn out to be a complete wild-goose chase. I could not be sure that Lauren had not made the whole thing up, but I had nothing to lose by trying. Her story was no crazier than mine, after all.

I wasn't quite sure how I was going to get him on his own with his brother and father in tow, but I would have to work that out on the day. At least it shouldn't be too difficult to find him. He had been tagged in a picture on Facebook standing in front of the bookies, so I knew exactly what he would be wearing in addition to what he looked like.

On the Sunday I made sure I checked the internet and memorised the names of all the winners. I was going to have to get myself on the road bright and early on Saturday morning. Racing started early at this time of the year in order to get all the races in before it got dark. I wanted to make sure I was at the track well before the first race at 12.10pm.

Unfortunately, there was one thing I hadn't taken into account and that was that not only did I not wake up until nearly 9am on Saturday morning, I also had a hangover. These were things that I had no control over, and as for the alarm clock by the side of my bed, it was about as much use to me as a chocolate teapot.

I had planned to get into Oxford early on Saturday morning and kit myself out with some suitable gear, perhaps a new Barbour jacket and some tweed trousers to make me look like a member of the racing fraternity, but there was no time for that now. In the end, I settled for a quick shower and a shave, and then put on an old suit that had been gathering dust in the wardrobe. The last thing I wanted to do was turn up looking scruffy and dishevelled: that wouldn't help me look convincing at all.

I didn't look too bad once I'd cleaned myself up, and apart from a fair bit of slow-moving traffic on the A40 heading out of Oxford, I managed to get to the track in plenty of time.

It was pretty busy at the course as I had expected for the main meeting on a Saturday, but there was plenty of room to move about. All I had to do now was to spot Josh and then work out a way to approach him.

It didn't take too long. I had decided to base myself in the stand above the betting ring so I could watch everyone coming and going. About five minutes before the first race, I spotted him, blond hair and long, black coat, just as I'd seen it on Facebook. In fact, as I watched he posed for the very picture I'd seen, his older-looking brother taking the snap and immediately uploading it.

I had already decided not to approach him before the first race, a novice hurdle event with only five runners. I knew that it was going to be won by a very short-priced favourite, ridden by the champion jockey, and that most of the punters on the track would have picked it. To go up to someone claiming to know the future and then tip them a 4/9F would be laughable.

After the race, in which the favourite duly obliged amid raucous cheers from the crowd, I followed Josh and his family inside where they headed straight for the bar. Josh's father looked quite pleased with himself as he ordered three pints of lager. He'd obviously lumped onto the winner, though he couldn't have won a fortune at the price. In contrast, Josh did not look pleased.

There were quite a few punters jostling for position at the bar. I had managed to manoeuvre myself in behind them, just as Josh's brother excused himself to go to the toilet. This gave me the opportunity I needed to squeeze myself in next to them at the bar where I caught Josh's eye. "Bit of a dead cert, that one, eh?" I said, hoping to spark off a bit of banter.

"That's what my dad said," replied Josh. "He had fifty quid on it. I went for the second favourite, though."

"I told you it was nailed on," said Josh's dad. "You wouldn't listen."

"Yeah, but I don't like backing horses at such short odds," replied Josh. "What you've won will barely cover the cost of these drinks. I want a bit of value."

"Value doesn't put food on the table, son. You'll learn," replied his dad. He was a big bloke, with plenty of muscle. I knew that he ran a building firm and it wasn't difficult to imagine him working on a building site. He also struck me as a bit of a know-it-all. Funnily enough, that was one of the things Lauren had said about Josh when she was listing her reasons for splitting up with him. Perhaps it ran in the family. Well, I certainly knew more about today's racing than either of them did. This was the ideal opportunity to set my plan in motion.

"Well, if it's value you're after, I've got a very decent priced selection for the next," I said. "Believe me, this one can't lose."

Josh's dad intervened. "Don't be fooled, son. Racecourses are full of people claiming to have inside information and giving out tips. I've heard it all before: take no notice."

"Sorry, mate, I should have introduced myself," I said, thinking quickly. "My name's Thomas Scott, I'm from Lambourn."

Josh's dad's ears perked up at this, "Geoff Gardner," he replied, "and this is my son, Josh. So, Lambourn, eh? I suppose you are going to tell me you know all the trainers?"

"Nothing like that," I replied. "But I do know which horse is going to win the next race. It's Mercury Wells, 8/1. Trust me."

"Experience has taught me not to trust people who say trust me," said Geoff, a cynical look on his face.

I held my ground and reiterated what I'd said before. "Look, believe me or not, I am telling you that Mercury Wells will win the next."

By now, they had got their drinks and the brother had returned.

"There's only four runners, Dad," said Josh. "Got to be worth a couple of quid, surely?"

"It's your funeral, son," said Geoff. "Nice to meet you, Thomas," he said, and then added sarcastically, "Give my love to everyone in Lambourn."

And with that they headed off outside to put their bets on for the next race. I followed at a discreet distance, trying not to be seen. What I was doing fell very much into the "stalker" category, and I didn't want them to get too suspicious.

The betting market for the race was dominated by the front two horses in the market but halfway round the favourite unseated his rider to groans from the crowd. The second favourite then got very tired in the heavy ground and was passed by Mercury Wells on the run-in.

Watching from afar, I was amused to see Geoff shouting "For fuck's sake" when the favourite fell, screwing up his ticket and throwing it to the ground. Josh, on the other hand, was jumping up and down cheering as Mercury Wells made the best of his way home. Everything was going according to plan, so as they headed back inside, I followed, ready to accost them again.

They sent Josh's brother to the bar, whilst they grabbed a seat in the corner and began poring over the *Racing Post*. I casually sauntered over to them, hoping that I might get a more friendly reaction from Geoff. However, it was the exact opposite. Far from congratulating me on my tip, Geoff was in a confrontational mood. "Oh, look, here he is," he sneered, as I approached "The champion tipster."

"What's the problem?" I asked. "I've just tipped you an 8/1 winner."

"You must think I was born yesterday, mate," responded Geoff. "Don't think I don't know your game."

"And what's that exactly?" I asked, wondering what he thought I was up to.

"It's the oldest trick in the book. You come and give us a tip for a race. Then you go round and find three other mugs and tip them a different horse each. You then go back to whoever you tipped the winning horse, tell them you have an even bigger cert for the next race, but you need to put the money on for them. Then we hand over our cash and you scarper."

"Did that happen to you once, then, Dad?" asked Josh. "Is that how you know?"

"No, son, I saw it in a film," replied Geoff, though I was sure I saw him turn a slightly deeper shade of red. I'd have bet good money that he hadn't seen it in a film. He must have been conned at some point in the past.

"I can assure you I am not going to ask you for any money," I replied. "But as it happens, I do know what is going to win the next race."

This was my big chance to really convince. The next race was a very competitive event, a handicap hurdle with sixteen runners which was going to be won by a rank outsider.

"Come on then, Prince Monolulu, what's the horse?" asked Geoff.

"Who's Prince Monolulu?" asked Josh.

"Never mind, before your time," said Geoff. "Ask your granddad."

Having no idea what he was talking about, I pressed on, and said, "If you really want to make some decent money today, put all your cash on Mister Fibuli."

"Now I know you're taking the piss," said Geoff. "That donkey is way past its best. It hasn't won for about three years."

"I'm telling you, Mister Fibuli is the one to be on. Back it, Josh. You backed that last one, didn't you?"

"I did," said Josh, "but Dad didn't. His horse fell."

"We've heard enough," said Geoff. "You are beginning to irritate me, mate. Come on, Josh, let's go and find something decent to bet on, and don't be wasting any money on any more of his duff tips. He just got lucky with that last one."

I let them go, but gave Josh a knowing look as he got up and mouthed "back it" at him. Then I retreated to a safe distance. Geoff looked like the sort of bloke who might be quite handy with his fists, and I didn't think winding him up any further would be the best course of action.

Ten minutes later, the crowd was stunned as Mister Fibuli, an eleven-year-old grey gelding, pulled clear of the field up the hill to win at odds of 33/1. Again I saw Josh celebrating, but there was a look of fury on Geoff's face. Josh's brother looked none too pleased either.

I didn't relish approaching them all again, so I loitered in the vicinity of the toilets and waited. The three of them were knocking back plenty of booze at the bar so they'd all have to pay a visit eventually. I stayed out of sight until Josh went in, and then followed him. He went up to the urinal and unzipped his flies, and I neatly slotted in next to him. This could easily have been misinterpreted by a casual observer, a middle-aged man hanging around outside the toilets and then following a young man in. I hadn't attracted any attention, though; everyone was too busy trying to work out the winner of the next race.

Now I was standing next to Josh who was in mid-piss: I had a captive audience so it was now or never.

"Mister Fibuli," I said. "What did I tell you?"

"Awesome tip, mate," said Josh. "I had a tenner on it. I got 50/1 with one bookie; most of them had it at 33/1. But you had better stay out of Dad's way: he's well annoyed with you. Where do you get your info from?" he asked.

I just came straight out with it "The future," I declared. "I'm a time traveller. I've come here specifically to meet you, because I've been given information that you are an expert on time travel and I am hoping that you can help me."

Josh seemed somewhat taken aback, but I certainly had his attention. "Who told you this?" he asked.

"I can't divulge that," I said, knowing that if I mentioned Lauren's name, it might have a negative effect. They had after all only recently split up. "But I do know the future, and I'll prove it once more," I said. "Back Hill Valley in the next, and when it wins, ditch your dad and brother and meet me in the on-course betting shop after the race."

Hill Valley won the handicap chase at odds of 5/1, and sure enough, Josh came and found me in the on-course betting shop. I had well and truly grabbed his attention, so I briefly outlined my situation to him. He was eager and attentive and seemed quite convinced.

"The thing is," he said, after I'd finished explaining, "I don't actually have the ability to travel where and when I want to in time, all I know is that it is possible. I am not sure exactly what I can do to help you."

"You may not have that ability now, but maybe you will one day in the future," I replied. "All I want to do is find out one thing – if the actions I am taking in my life lead to a happy ever after." I want to know that in a decade or more from now, I haven't died of cancer, my wife is alive and well, and that Stacey is happy."

"And you want me to find this out for you?" asked Josh.

"If you can," I replied. "And if you ever do find out how to do it, come back in time and tell me."

"When?" said Josh.

"Not now," I said. "Earlier, much earlier, when I've done all the things I need to do to put life on the track that I want."

I had already worked all this out in my head. It needed to be way back, when I was a young man, before I had even met Sarah. I took a betting slip from the counter, grabbed a small blue pen, and wrote the following down on the slip:

*Thomas Scott. 6th August 1990, 5pm, Radcliffe Camera.*

I had picked out this date more or less at random. I had made it as late in the day as possible as I couldn't be sure exactly where I would be in the morning. This would give me plenty of time to get there in case I woke up and found myself out of town. The Radcliffe Camera was a well-known monument in the centre of the city, and seemed as good a place as any.

Before I gave the slip to him I also wrote down my date of birth and home address.

"Keep hold of that," I said, handing it to him. "You should be able to find out all you need about me from those details. Meanwhile, I will be there on that date and at that time. If there is any way you can find a way to make it back there, please do."

Josh pocketed the betting slip. "This is surreal," he said, "but if I can be there, I will."

"Thanks," I said. "And now you'd better get back to the others. And don't forget to back Henry Clare in the next. A bit of extra cash towards your time travel experiments wouldn't go amiss, I'm sure."

"Thank-you," said Josh, "in more ways than one. You've inspired me. I'm determined to unlock the secret of time travel."

"See you in 1990 then," I replied, more in hope than expectation, and we parted company. I didn't bother hanging around for the rest of the meeting, I felt satisfied that my work for the day was done, and I didn't really want to run into Josh's dad again. All I had to do now was to wait a couple of decades to see if he turned up or not.

### July 2021

My day at the races had given me a bit of a taste for gambling, so I decided to amuse myself with it a while longer. Even if I couldn't make any long-term benefit from it, I could still have some fun on a daily basis. I also wanted to ensure Stacey was well taken care of in the future, so I decided it might be fun to engineer a lottery win on her behalf.

I waited until a rollover Saturday arrived to ensure I'd have the only winning ticket, and tempted Stacey to spend the evening at home with the offer of a Chinese takeaway. She adored Chinese food, so it wasn't difficult to persuade her.

The summer had seen a change take place in my domestic circumstances. It had been in August that Stacey had moved in with

David in his flat in London. She'd found it a tough break to make, and on the day she left there had been tears, her saying that she was worried about leaving me all alone. I assured her that this wasn't going to be a problem, wished her well, and watched as she and David drove away to start their life together. She had promised that she would visit me every other weekend and, true to her word, she had done.

Having Stacey back home with me brought a new lease of life to the old house. It had other benefits, too. I had reason to make more of an effort with cooking, and began to enjoy eating with her three or four nights a week. Sometimes we would just stay in and watch TV together; other nights she was out with David, or he would come over and stay with us. She seemed blissfully happy, and it was no surprise when she broached the subject of moving in with him.

It was while she was plucking up the courage to tell me she would be moving out that I got the first indication that there may have been some stormy waters in the past.

"Dad, I'm so happy with David," she had said. "I wasn't sure if I'd ever feel comfortable with someone after what happened when I was sixteen, but he's been so good to me."

This set alarm bells ringing, but I could hardly blatantly come out and ask her what had happened when she was sixteen. It was clearly a "big thing" that I obviously should have known about. Up until that moment it had never been referred to before. There would be plenty of time to find out. Stacey was 21 now, so I just replied that I was glad she had found someone to make her happy.

So now, here we were, on Saturday night, and I was about to make her even happier. I'd made sure that we were sitting down watching the *Lotto* draw as we ate our Chinese. I'd even put a bottle of champagne in the fridge ready for the ensuing celebration.

Just before the draw, I said, "Oh, yes, I've just remembered, I've bought you a present," and handed her the £2 ticket.

"This is a surprise," she remarked, "I can't remember you ever playing the Lotto before. Why now?"

"I don't know really," I said, "I was just passing the newsagent's in Summertown earlier and thought, why not? I knew you were coming round tonight so thought it might be a bit of fun."

It was soon more than a bit of fun as the first three numbers came out of the ball machine, matching three numbers on our ticket.

"We've got three numbers," said Stacey, excitedly. "That's worth about £25, isn't it?"

"We've got four now," I said, as the number 44 plopped down out of the machine.

"Oh my God," mouthed Stacey, watching, as the fifth ball, number 12, appeared. "We could win this."

The last ball seemed to take ages to appear. We were waiting on number 5. I tried to seem as excited as Stacey was, but it was difficult to fake it. When you knew the result in advance, it took away the suspense. Sure enough, number 5 appeared and Stacey started jumping up and down and screaming "We've won, we've won! I can't believe it!"

Caught up in the moment of euphoria, I grabbed the bottle of champagne from the fridge and popped it open. Stacey was in a state of shock and disbelief, but there was no denying the evidence on the ticket.

Once she'd calmed down sufficiently, she phoned David, who was down in London. In barely an hour, his car was pulling up outside. A call to the claim line confirmed we did indeed have the only winning ticket, and were some £5 million or more better off than we had been that morning.

The celebrations went on long into the night. We sat around the kitchen table, booze flowing freely, talking about what we'd do with the money.

I knew it was of no benefit to me where I was going, so I made my intentions clear. "Stacey, I bought the ticket for you, I want you to have the money. You've been talking about moving in with David in London. Now you can buy yourself a nice house there and not have to worry about rent or a mortgage ever again."

Houses in London didn't come cheap. I'd read in the paper that the average price in most areas was now well over a million pounds. In areas such as Kensington and Chelsea it was several million.

"All I ask is that you look after me in my old age," I said, wondering if I'd done enough yet by keeping off the cigarettes to have earned an old age.

Up until now, any changes I had made in the world hadn't affected our lives directly. Buying the lottery ticket was the first major change I had instigated. From now on, the timeline was certain to diverge from the one I had known before. Stacey and David were wealthy now and I hoped that this change would be for better, rather than for worse. I knew that money didn't necessarily buy happiness and they had that already. If I had any doubts about him or his motives, I wouldn't have done it. But I had already seen that he had looked after my daughter well for several years when he was the one bringing in the bulk of their earnings. I knew him well enough to know that he wouldn't want to be with her now just because she was rich.

So that was another timeline potentially in existence, one where Stacey had won the lottery, as opposed to the one where she hadn't. Whether the original timeline had now vanished, or if it would be just another duplicate I still had no way of telling. It was more important now that I looked to the past to find out what had happened to Stacey when she was sixteen and try to put it right.

# Indulgence

**June 2021**

Stacey graduated in June which meant that she was soon to leave me again, heading back to university in Southampton for her final term. This was to form the pattern of the next three years: her spending holidays with me, and term times away.

To pass some time, I decided to have a bit of fun with the horse racing again. One of the bookmakers that advertised on television was currently running an advertising campaign that I found incredibly irritating. I had also heard that this particular bookmaker was notorious for banning or restricting horse racing punters who dared to have the audacity to back more than their fair share of winners. So one Monday, forearmed with the knowledge of the day's results, I decided to have a little fun at their expense.

I went into one of their betting shops in a town a few miles away from Oxford and placed a £10 accumulator on six horses running that afternoon. I'd worked out that the accumulative odds of the starting prices of these horses would add up to just under £1,000,000. This was the maximum limit that the bookmaker offered for winnings on horse racing.

After I put the money on, I found myself a comfy chair and waited for the action to unfold. I more or less had the place to myself. Other than a couple of pensioners betting rip-off forecasts on the lunchtime dog races, and a few depressed-looking men pouring money into the roulette machines, the place was deserted.

Nobody took a lot of notice of me, as the first two horses duly won at odds of 2/1 and 5/1. It probably wasn't that unusual for a punter to get two winners up like that. The bored-looking girl behind the counter seemed oblivious to what was going on. However, after the third horse had won at 20/1, I saw her looking at me, and she called her manager out from the office to look at something on the computer. Clearly, the bet had been flagged up as one with potential liabilities.

I had £3780 going on to the next horse at 9/1. When this went in, my winnings had risen to £37,800. The manager came out from behind the counter.

"Is this your bet, sir?" he asked.

"Yes," I said. "There's not a problem, is there?

"Not at all," he said, cheerfully. "I just like to get to know my customers," he said.

A couple of other punters were nosing around now to see what was happening. The shop had got progressively busier as the afternoon had worn on.

"What's the craic, here?" asked one, a pensioner with an Irish accent.

I thought I'd let the punters join in the fun, why not? "Oh, I've got an accumulator running up," I said. "First four have gone in already."

"How much has he got to come, Brian?" asked another, who reminded me a bit of Josh's dad.

"I can't tell you that, client confidentiality," said the manager, as he headed back behind the counter. He didn't seem remotely bothered by proceedings. It wasn't his money after all: he was just an employee. I guessed his superiors at head office were already aware of my bet. Presumably all of the tills were linked up via the internet.

"It's alright, I don't mind," I said, and showed the punters the slip.

"Blimey, you've got thousands running up here," said the Geoff lookalike. "Hey, Nobby, come and have a look at this." He gestured to a smartly dressed man with a small beard who just happened to be carrying a small pocket calculator. "Nobby will work it out for you."

I'd already worked it out, but Nobby glanced at the slip, then at the screen and without resorting to his calculator said, "Bloody hell, you've got £37,800 running up here," loudly enough for the remainder of the shop's punters to gather round. They had a sniff of a possible big win and were all right behind me. Perhaps they wanted to unite behind one of their number who might be about to strike a major blow at their old enemy. More likely it was just because they were hoping I might splash some of the winnings their way if the bet came off.

I had no reason to suspect that the bet would not pay off; however, I was about to discover that not everything I read in the following day's papers was set in stone. The fifth horse duly won, generating much excitement from the shop's punters who sensed they might be witnessing a once-in-a-lifetime moment, but something was wrong. I clearly recalled the price of the horse being

4/1 when I'd memorised the results from the paper, but when the starting prices were returned from the course, the official price was 3/1.

What was happening here? Had I made a mistake? It turned out that I had, but it wasn't my memory that was in error.

As the last race approached, all eyes were on the screen to see what price my last selection would be. It had £151,200 going onto it, though it should have been £189,000. I clearly remembered that my final horse, Hot Girl, had also started at 4/1, but I could see as the race approached that it was going to start at nowhere near that price. It opened at 7/4 on course and the price instantly began to drop, to 6/4, and then 5/4.

Unlike the other punters who were in a major state of excitement, Nobby was frowning and shaking his head.

"You know what you've done wrong here, don't you?" he asked.

"No, not really," I said. "But I'm sure you're going to tell me."

"You didn't take the prices on any of these horses, you've just let them run at SP. Hot Girl was 5/1 this morning, if you had taken that price, you'd be looking at nearly a million quid now."

"I was sure Hot Girl would have been a bigger price than this," I replied. "I thought it would start at about 4/1."

"And it probably would have done," replied Nobby, "if it hadn't been for this bet. The bookies won't be worried about whether your horse wins or not. They will have sent all the money back to the course or backed it on the exchanges to drive the price down as low as they can. In fact, I wouldn't put it past them to stop it winning altogether."

"Does that happen?" I asked.

"Some people think so," said Nobby. "There was a big scandal about it years ago with a number of jockeys arrested. But it hasn't happened recently. It would probably be a lot harder to get away with it these days, what with the technology and everything. And they can hedge anything at a bigger price on the exchanges anyway, so they will probably end up making a profit whatever happens."

This interesting development in the conversation was cut short by the start of the race. Word seemed to have got around the local punting fraternity and a sizeable crowd had gathered in the shop now to cheer Hot Girl on. It was a five-furlong handicap and it didn't take more than about a minute to run. Thankfully, Nobby's conspiracy theories about the horse being stopped proved to be unfounded, and Hot Girl did indeed win amid much cheering, but the starting price was a huge disappointment. Hot Girl was returned at 4/5, which gave me a grand total of £272,160. Not anything like as much as I had hoped, but a sizeable sum nonetheless.

Unfortunately it was a sum I was not going to be able to lay my hands on. Amid the celebrations and congratulations from the shop's punters, I made my way to the till. Up until now, I hadn't really thought about how I might collect the money, but it was more problematical than I'd thought.

"Yeah, they shortened that up, alright," said Nobby. "Just like when Frankie landed his magnificent seven."

"Congratulations," said the manager, who had joined the rest of us in front of the big screen. He seemed as delighted as everybody else. If what Nobby had said was true, his firm had probably done quite nicely out of this. He then added, "I'm not going to be able to pay you out until tomorrow, though."

Obviously I wasn't expecting him to have a quarter of a million quid just sitting in the safe, but I had hoped that I might be able to get a bank transfer or a good old-fashioned cheque.

"I don't have the authority to pay out a win for this amount," he explained, "but someone from Head Office is coming down tomorrow, and they will present you with the cheque. If you don't mind, we'd like to get a photographer and a couple of journalists along to cover the story."

"No can do, I'm afraid," I said, quickly thinking up a plausible lie. "I've got to fly to the States on business tonight and I won't be back for a month."

I considered the situation, and then decided I knew what I was going to do. It was time to do a good deed for the day. "I've got a suggestion," I said. "Can we go somewhere private?"

He took me into his office, and I explained what I wanted to do. I then gave him all of my contact details, name and address, and wrote out detailed instructions in a letter, signed it, and left it with him.

If they did contact me to confirm all this, hopefully my future self in this timeline would verify it. I'd instructed him to send £125,000 to the Injured Jockeys Fund, £125,000 to the RSPCA, with the remainder to be shared amongst the shop's staff and punters.

Happy that I'd given something back to all those involved in putting on the daily sport of kings, I left the shop, head held high, good deed for the day well and truly done.

### April 2021

After my memorable experience in the betting shop that afternoon, I only went back a couple more times. I restricted myself to more realistic targets on those subsequent visits, putting on bets that paid out more modest sums like £3,000, but even that proved problematical to get my hands on. There always seemed to be some sort of issue. Either they didn't have enough money in the shop and the bank was closed, or they did have the money but it was in a time-locked safe that wouldn't open for another hour. In the end I grew rather bored of it: there was no real thrill in the gamble when there was no risk involved, and it was a waste of time waiting around to get paid, so I decided to try another tactic.

As far as I could see, the only way to get a large wad of cash from a bookmaker was to go on-course to a big meeting and bet in cash. It was very handy if I wanted to get hold of a large sum of money for use specifically on that day. Despite the world in general shifting money around electronically via plastic, on-course bookmakers still preferred to deal in cash. Using the winnings to buy material objects was a waste of time, but what I could buy was experiences. Any money that I laid my hands on came with a strict "expires at 3am" stipulation.

I got into the habit of starting the afternoon with a visit to a racecourse, usually one not too far from London, such as Sandown Park or Ascot. I would take £10,000 or more in cash from the on-course bookmaker's satchels and then head into London to enjoy some of the finer things in life.

I booked myself into the penthouse suites of some of the city's most expensive hotels. I dined in three-starred Michelin restaurants, washing down my gourmet dinners with the most expensive wine and champagne I could lay my hands on.

I also got to indulge myself in every sexual fantasy I could ever ask for. My fling with Lauren had given me a taste for sex yet all the same restrictions I'd had before on my sex life still prevailed. Once again it seemed I had no choice but to resort to prostitutes. My experience in Milton Keynes was long behind me. Now I could afford to pay for the very highest-class escorts. After all, what was the point in sitting in these expensive restaurants and hotels like some Billy-no-mates? Consequently, I always made sure that I arranged a suitable companion for the evening.

These were classy, elegant, well dressed girls who looked a million dollars. I made sure I looked the part, too. On one of my first visits to London I had found a suit in an upmarket store that fitted me as well as if it were tailor-made. With a shirt and tie plus new shoes to go with it, not to mention an extremely expensive watch, I walked around oozing class and wealth. To get by in London, you didn't just need to have money, you needed to show you had it. Walking around looking the part, I found that few doors were closed to me.

Some of the hotels found it a little odd when I paid for the rooms in cash, but no questions were ever asked.

After a few visits I had my routine off to a T. Go to the track, stash the cash, and take a taxi straight into London, arranging my "date" for the night on the way. I'd head straight for the store where it was easy to get myself kitted out – I knew where everything was so just bought the same things straight off the peg every time. I must have bought that suit 50 times over. It was the ultimate in repeat business for the store. Usually by 5pm I'd be safely ensconced in some luxury suite somewhere looking forward to an evening of the best pleasures money could buy.

My indulgences grew and grew. Sometimes I'd order two girls together and then we'd really have a party. Aged 50 and acting like a playboy, some might have looked at me and seen a man having a mid-life crisis. I preferred to see it more as a young man sowing his wild oats and getting it all out of his system before marriage and parenthood beckoned. I already had Stacey with me during the holidays, and it wouldn't be too much longer until she was back with me full-time. Then I would "grow up" and become a responsible adult.

Even now, it wasn't debauched champagne orgies all the time. If Stacey was at home, often I'd go into London after the races and buy the most luxurious delicacies I could find and take them home to Oxford for the evening. So we dined on everything from Beluga caviar to Wagyu steak. One time I even brought home a 7kg Ibérico ham I had seen hanging in the food hall at Harrods. It cost over £2,000 and was the most delicious thing I had ever tasted.

It was in booze where I really excelled. I found an antique wine dealer in London and frequently brought home a bottle that had cost me over £10,000. As with the suit, it was often the same one. There were only about twenty of these bottles left in the world, apparently, but I must have drunk that particular one at least that number of times myself. Stacey had no idea of the value of the wine she was enthusiastically glugging down beside me. To have told her would only have raised awkward questions. Officially I was well off, but not that well off.

So that was my life in 2021, a carefree paradise where I could have whatever I wanted. I enjoyed it tremendously for several months, but in the end it began to lose its appeal. For all my fun and games, and despite the fact that I had Stacey, I felt lonely and as if my life lacked direction. As 2021 gave way to 2020 there were changes on the horizon that I hoped would remedy that.

# Work

**October 2020**

My big "Five-O" was approaching, a landmark birthday. For many, this marked the turning point from the last gasp of youth into middle age. I was more than happy to be going the other way, having seen some significant improvements in my appearance over the past couple of years. Despite still being fat, my hair was growing quite encouragingly. The bald patch in the middle was noticeably smaller and there were some welcome flecks of black appearing amongst the grey.

I had a few minor health niggles that I was hoping would disappear as time went by. My eyesight without my glasses was abysmal so I went into Specsavers to try and find out more about my optical history. I was pleased to discover that I'd only had to start wearing glasses in my mid-forties.

My teeth weren't in particularly good shape and I'd lost two of my rear molars in the past year. One of these caused me no end of aggravation at the time. I had to go to the dentist three days running on emergency appointments to have the same tooth removed, such was my pain on awaking each morning with the rotten tooth in my mouth. It was all very well drinking the same expensive bottle of wine several times, but repeating the dentist experience was something I could have done without. On the third day I stuck a quid under the pillow before I went to bed, figuring I must be in debt to the tooth fairy. It was gone in the morning, but the tooth was back. She must have waved her magic wand, because the pain had thankfully subsided enough on that fourth morning for me to cope with it.

My birthday was on the 21st of October and it coincided with another milestone event, my retirement from the retailer I had been with for over 25 years. Since leaving, I had been out for a drink with Nick a couple of times, which had enabled me to find out more about my past career.

We had both started in the mid-1990s working in a flagship superstore outside Oxford. I had been a supervisor in-store, whilst he was a manager in the warehouse. We'd worked our way up together, gaining jobs at Head Office early in the new millennium and climbing the corporate ladder.

By 2017 I had been promoted to Marketing Director. However, it seemed that things had rather gone to pieces after Sarah's death.

I had taken her death very hard, understandably, and had been given some compassionate leave afterwards. I found it difficult to get the precise details out of Nick, as clearly he felt uncomfortable talking about it. Reading between the lines, it was clear that my heart had no longer been in it when I went back to work.

A difficult trading climate, poor results and a new CEO meant that I was allowed to leave gracefully in 2020. In other words, in recognition of my years of good service, I'd been offered a golden handshake and a comfortable pension as a polite way of saying "piss off". It sounded like a reasonable enough deal to me. I'd been left with enough money to live on for the rest of my life hence my apparent lack of interest in getting another job in the years that followed. That wasn't to say that I hadn't been offered plenty. A number of headhunters had rung up to try and tempt me into a new position during the 2020s, but I had turned them all down in this life, presumably just as I had in my previous one.

My reluctance to return to work left one nagging doubt in my mind. Could it be that my lack of activity and direction in the years following my retirement had been contributory factors in my death? It may not all have been down to the purely physical causes of my cancer, such as smoking. Had my body, sensing that my mind had given up, also decided to give up? I had heard stories about people who had lost the will to live in such a way after the death of a partner, following them to the grave soon after.

Perhaps this was something else I could change. If I saved Sarah, perhaps I would save myself. It was less than three years now until her date with destiny. Until then, it was time to leave my retirement behind and see what working life had to offer.

My last day at work had taken place on Friday the 23rd of October, but a "surprise" lay in store for me on the Saturday evening. My friends and family had arranged a joint 50th birthday/retirement party for me at a local hotel. They had no doubt done a fantastic job of keeping it a secret from me. However, not knowing of my backwards existence, no one thought to keep it a secret afterwards.

Having seen all the pictures on Facebook and hearing Stacey and David enthusing about what a great night it had been, I was quite looking forward to it. Judging by the horrific hangover I woke up with on the Sunday morning, it must have been a good one.

On the day of the party, I played suitably dumb about the whole thing, allowing Stacey and David to believe they had duped me into thinking we were going to the hotel for a meal. When we arrived and went into the suite where the party was to take place I did my bit to feign surprise. In fact, there was a surprise waiting for me, and that was the sheer scale of the events. I was amazed at just how many people were there, it must have been well over a hundred and they all seemed genuinely delighted to see me.

I had become so used to living as a social recluse over the past few years that it came as quite a shock to realise just how many friends I apparently had. But where had they been in the years that followed? Was this what happened to people when they got older, or left work? Did they just fade into obscurity? Other than Nick, very few people had kept in touch, a couple of Christmas cards, and that was about it.

I spent the evening getting to know as many people as I could. I found putting names to faces quite difficult at the best of times, but to avoid future embarrassment I made a huge effort to try and remember as many as possible. I also met some family members I hadn't seen before, a couple of cousins and an ancient uncle who spent the whole evening complaining that he had to go outside to smoke his pipe.

Stacey had hired a DJ who was about my age, and he was playing an excellent set. Clearly he'd been told beforehand about my musical tastes. I'm glad someone had, because I still didn't know what a lot of them were myself at this point. I had been working my way through some of the playlists on my iPod but even so, I got to hear a lot of tunes that were new to me that night, and very agreeable. As he played some classic old skool dance hits from the 90s I invariably found myself drawn towards the dance floor.

"Remember this one?" Nick called across at me, also on the dance floor. "Takes you back, doesn't it? Ibiza '98? Those were the days!"

I'd never heard the tune before, which I figured by the lyrics was probably called *Horny*, but I knew all about Ibiza '98. Nick had been reminiscing about it one night when we had been in the pub. It had been the holiday of a lifetime for us at the time, not to mention a milestone moment in my life as well. It was on that holiday that I'd first met Sarah.

I really got into the party atmosphere as the night wore on. Up on the dance floor, in the multicoloured beams of light casting patterns across the room, I heard the soundtrack of my life played out. Many of the songs, even if unfamiliar now, I sensed had had special meaning to me at certain points in my life. From the dance floor fillers to the early 90s indie rock and Britpop, I was enjoying every moment. For the first time since my new life had begun back in that hospital bed in 2025, I really began to feel like I had a place in the world.

I had another pleasant surprise at the end of the evening. A red-headed beauty with a dress to match her strawberry blonde curls grabbed hold of me when the smoochy numbers came on and led me to the dance floor. I'd been introduced to her earlier as "Carol", and I knew that she worked with me in my office. She was younger than me, mid-thirties at a guess and being dragged onto the dance floor by her was a major ego boost.

On the floor she wrapped her arms around me and, with her head on my shoulder, said into my ear, "All these years we've worked together, Tom, and I've never had the courage to tell you this until now, but I bloody fancy the arse off you."

I pulled back a little to look at her face, which was just crying out to be kissed, and leaned in instinctively. Well, why not? It was a lovely, romantic snog, without any sexual overtones, just full of affection. This was something my life had lacked. Contrary to popular opinion, most of the escorts I had been with in London had kissed, but that was a mere prelude to sex and it had all been fake anyway. As for Lauren, she hadn't seemed particular interested in kissing at all, always wanting to get straight down to the action.

Kissing Carol was the first time I think I had felt genuine affection from a woman. Later I would find out more about the years we worked together, confirming that nothing like this had happened between us before. Perhaps that could change.

"Will you call me?" she asked tentatively.

"Of course," I said. But clearly I wouldn't be able to and perhaps my other self in my former timeline hadn't either, as I had no inkling that any of this had occurred until today. She hadn't attempted to contact me either, so perhaps this little romantic moment hadn't occurred in the original version of this day. It didn't matter one way or the other: all I knew was that I had a good friend here, whether I managed to take it further in the past or not.

I hadn't been too sure how I was going to handle work. In fact, I had been dreading it, but meeting so many of my colleagues that night had certainly helped. Before the party there had only been Nick, but now there was Carol and others, too. As long as I could bluff my way through the first few days I didn't see any reason why I couldn't pull it off, even if I was going in completely cold. It was going to be the ultimate case of on-the-job training and I'd just have to figure it all out as I went along.

There was no obligation to go in at all really. After all, I could just phone in sick anytime I fancied a day off. It would only be one day, as in theory I'd go back in the next day. I could do it every single day if I wanted to, and carry on as before, but quite honestly I'd had enough of that. Now I'd met Carol, I wanted to get to know her and have some proper human interaction. I was not going to get that sitting around the house all day in my underpants watching old quiz shows on a channel I'd discovered called *Challenge*.

So, on the day following my party, I dug out my old suit that I had not worn since my trip to Cheltenham, and headed off in the company BMW to work. This had rather impressively appeared out of nowhere on my driveway that morning. Presumably, with it being my last day I was going to have to give it back. I'd been managing without a car for quite a while now. It seemed I'd gone almost two years without one before I bought the Mercedes.

It was cold and raining, and the traffic around the Oxford Ring Road was horrendous. Eventually, I pulled into the driveway of the aging and ugly office block which had served as the company's Head Office since the 1960s. Then I realised I had a problem, the sort of thing I was always running into. The entrance to the car park was controlled by a barrier which was opened using a keypad which meant yet another PIN number that I didn't know. I pressed the button to call security and got a rather angry-sounding response from the other end.

"Is that you, again, Scott?" bellowed a voice out of the speaker. "You'd forget your bloody head if it wasn't screwed on."

"Yeah, sorry," I meekly responded. "I can't seem to remember my entry code." There must be a camera somewhere, but I couldn't see it. How else would he have known it was me?

"How long have you worked here?" he replied. "Too long, I reckon. I think it's time you retired. In fact, I'm personally going to chuck you out myself at the end of the day."

With that, the intercom cut off, and the barrier went up. Unfortunately for me, I was soon to face the same problem when I reached the entry door to discover another keypad blocking my way.

I pressed the button again, and a large man, roughly mid-fifties and dressed in a security uniform, appeared in the doorway looking furious. There were no prizes for deducing that this was the same man who had spoken to me before. I later discovered that his name was Barry and he used to be a sergeant major in the Army before retiring and taking this job. As I was soon to learn, he kept up a constant stream of banter with everyone and, despite his belligerent behaviour, was a hugely popular character around the building.

"I'll swing for you, Scott, I really will," he said as he opened the door. "I'm not surprised they bloody sacked you, how are you supposed to run a multinational corporation when you can't even open the fucking door? No wonder the share price has gone to shit."

I retorted lamely with the first load of drivel that came into my head. "We are busy making all sorts of crucial business decisions every day at board level, you know. Remembering trivia like the key code to get into the building isn't that high on my list of priorities, I'm afraid."

"Don't make me laugh," said Barry. "I bet you don't even know how much a tin of beans costs in one of your shops. I suppose you want me to let you through the internal door as well?"

"Please," I replied, and he swiped a card through a feeder on the edge of the keypad.

"Unbelievable!" exclaimed Barry, theatrically, and then turned his attention back towards the main door as a young woman entered, dressed rather glamorously. As I went through the internal door I heard Barry giving her some stick.

"What on earth have you got on today?" I heard him ask. "This isn't a fashion show, you know. And where's your coat? Summer's finished, in case you hadn't noticed."

The door closed behind me. Chuckling, I made my way along the corridor, hoping I'd be able to find my way to my office. All I'd managed to find out from some subtle questioning on Saturday night was that it was on the second floor, so I took the lift at the end of the corridor and trusted to luck.

The lift doors opened out at level 2 into a small communal area by the entrance to a modern-looking café. I noticed one or two vaguely familiar faces around from the party and was very relieved to see Nick queuing up to get a drink. He spotted me and called over, "Hey, Tom, fancy a coffee?"

From there it was plain sailing. I asked him if he'd walk back to my office with me, making sure he led the way.

"Catch you later," said Nick, when we got there. "I've got a meeting to get to." I was on my own now, but reasonably confident I could bluff my way through.

The marketing department was a large, open-plan area with individual work areas laid out in small cubicles, nicknamed "pig-pens" by the employees. I recognised most of the staff here from the party, but couldn't put names to faces, despite my best attempts to remember. Fortunately, I didn't have to. The company had been thoughtful enough to install nameplates above each pig-pen, which gave not only the names of people but also their job titles, which was extremely helpful.

Everyone seemed very pleased to see me. Whether that was because I was popular or because they were pleased it was my last day, I couldn't tell. At least the nameplates meant that I could call people by name, with only the odd slip. If people stuck to their own desks, I wouldn't have had to have gone through the following exchange:

"Morning, Tom," said one.

"Morning, Roger!" I replied, enthusiastically.

"I'm not Roger, I'm Philip," said the man. "Roger's not in today!"

"I know," I replied. "It was a joke. I thought when I came in, Roger looks different today!"

"That old chestnut," replied Philip, laughing. "I'm going to miss you, mate," he said.

Cheered that he seemed to genuinely like me, and pleased that my quick thinking had got me out of trouble, I headed towards the door impressively marked *Thomas Scott – Marketing Director* and went inside. Having my own office whilst everyone else was out in the pig-pens was good: it meant I could hide away from any difficult situations. I think I was going to enjoy being a big cheese.

So, all was well. I had got through the most difficult bit. A quick call to the IT helpline to plead ignorance of my password soon had it reset and I was up and running. My glittering career in the retail industry was underway.

**April 2020**

Six months had passed and I had sailed along in my new role with ease. My computer had emails going back years, and documents galore that taught me everything I needed to know to do my job.

In fact, I didn't even need to do that much. "Never put off until tomorrow what you can do today" worked nicely in reverse for me. The phrase "I'll get back to you tomorrow on that" became my standard response to anything that wasn't life-threateningly urgent, i.e. pretty much everything.

I soon banished my earlier thoughts about phoning in sick on a regular basis, because I actually quite enjoyed going to work. The daily banter with Barry on security was always good value, and now that I had inside information that Carol fancied me, I took every opportunity to flirt with her. Supposedly that was breaking one of the cardinal rules. Not only were we colleagues, but I was her boss as well. She sat just across from my office in a pig-pen by the window where she performed her role as marketing manager for health and beauty products. I spent many an hour when I was supposed to be working gazing across at her slim, sexy figure, imagining what her gorgeous red curls would look like cascading down over her breasts as she eagerly rode me to orgasm. It was hardly surprising I never got any work done.

    I decided that I would definitely shag her if I got the opportunity, and thankfully one presented itself just after Easter. One of the great things about my job was the foreign travel it brought with it. Our company had expanded all over Europe and we had stores in most countries, as well as a regional office. My role meant that I was frequently required to attend meetings in several of Europe's capitals. It was not unusual at all for me to find myself waking up in a swanky hotel in some famous city on the continent, giving me the ideal opportunity to do some sightseeing.

    If I was lucky enough to have already concluded my business the previous day, I'd just contrive a reason to miss my return flight and stay in the city for the day. Over the course of the year, I got to visit the Colosseum, check out the red-light district in Amsterdam, and drink coffee on the banks of the Seine. Life was good.

    It was on the latter visit that I got the chance to get up close and personal with Carol. We were in Paris for two nights for a meeting with a new perfume supplier who wanted us to stock their fragrance in our UK stores. Although I woke up alone in my hotel, a very upmarket establishment close to the Eiffel Tower, on the day we were due to fly back I had plans to change all of that.

So the previous day, I decided that I was going to woo Carol. I could hardly be better placed to do it. Paris in the springtime was a beautiful place. Once our business was successfully concluded for the day, I suggested that we go out for the evening and find the best restaurant we could to celebrate closing the deal.

We found a lovely old-fashioned little boutique restaurant with red and white-checked tablecloths, bread served in baskets, and a superb view of the Eiffel Tower in the setting sun.

We sat, drank champagne, and talked about our lives deep into the night. The restaurant didn't rush us and I could gladly have stayed all night in her company, but eventually, stuffed with food, drink and coffee we almost fell out onto the pavement. We were laughing and drunk, not just from the alcohol, but from the high spirits that only an evening in perfect company can provide.

Our route back to the hotel took us directly past the Eiffel Tower. As we walked close by, I slipped my hand into hers. She seemed surprised, but not in a negative way.

"You've never done that before," she said.

"Well, I've never been with you in the most romantic city in the world before," I replied, and turned to her in the shadow of Paris's most famous landmark and kissed her full on the lips. She responded enthusiastically, her tongue probing its way into my mouth. After that, we couldn't get back to the hotel quickly enough and were soon tearing our clothes off each and flinging them across the room.

It was one glorious night of passion, which more than lived up to my office fantasies. Sadly, it was one that I never did get the chance to repeat, as the opportunity never really arose again. In fact, although I didn't know it at the time, this was to be my final liaison before married life beckoned. I was really glad that it had been such a memorable one.

# Sarah

**March 2018**

The two years following my romantic interlude with Carol in Paris passed relatively uneventfully. I enjoyed the social life and travel that my newfound vocation brought, whilst continuing to skilfully avoid doing any actual work.

The weekly planning meetings were a source of much amusement to me. It was full of young graduate trainees all clamouring to impress me. They were incredibly eager to get their voices heard and climb the corporate ladder, but I just found them irritating. Kissing the boss's arse and asking as many knowledgeable-sounding questions might have worked on some people, but I saw right through the falseness.

There was a general sense of panic around the building due to the dire times that the company had fallen on in recent years. After decades of being one of the major food retailers in the country, the 2010s had brought one crisis after another. A surge of popularity for foreign discount chains undercutting prices had seen many former loyal customers desert our stores in droves. Various food scares and other scandals had dogged not just us, but the other big retailers as well. Most of them were also struggling, but not as badly as us.

To try and combat the decline, it seemed we had launched all manner of initiatives, none of which seemed to have made any difference. So now, in these weekly meetings, my eager young charges competed desperately, trying to be the one to come up with the genius idea that would turn the company's fortunes around.

Listening to the various suggestions it seemed to me that we had completely lost sight of the golden rule of focusing on the customer. Everything seemed to be about money and manipulation – coming up with clever promotional ideas that worked well on paper, but were insulting to the customer's intelligence. The whole BOGOF (Buy One, Get One Free) offer had been completely abused in recent years. Once a great way of giving customers fantastic deals, it had been cynically manipulated to try and trick the shoppers into believing they were getting a bargain when they weren't.

Modern shoppers weren't falling for it. They were more clued up than ever before, thanks to price comparison sites and other resources. They didn't like being taken for mugs and voted with their feet, heading off to the discount stores instead.

Most of the ideas that were brought up in the meetings were just variations on the same old themes. Sometimes I decided to take the piss and throw in an utterly ludicrous idea to see what the reaction would be.

"I know," I said, one summer morning when I would much rather have been elsewhere. "Why don't we forget about tired old BOGOFs and introduce Buy One Get Three Free instead? That will pull them in. No one's ever done that before. We could do it on say, blocks of cheese. All we have to do is raise the price of the cheese from say, £3 a block to £10 and we'll be laughing. They'll be getting four for a tenner, but they'll think they are getting the bargain of a lifetime!"

It was a ridiculous suggestion. Although there might be the odd idiot who would think it was cheap, the vast majority of the general public would see through such a blatant con immediately. And who would want to buy four blocks of cheese at one time anyway? However, since I was the boss and I'd suggested it, all the sycophants in the room were eagerly nodding and agreeing. I was surrounded by yes-men and yes-women.

The only exception was Carol, who had a disapproving look on her face, and when she questioned me about it later, I admitted I had said it for a joke. I was impressed with her for challenging me. I liked people who didn't follow the herd.

From March 2018 I found I was no longer required in work. I had been given three months' compassionate leave following Sarah's death. People had been very sympathetic on my return and even Barry had been nice for a day or two. It was just as well, really, as I had been waking up most days with an absolutely stinking hangover. Clearly booze had been my way of blotting out the pain. On the plus side, my tobacco cravings had more or less disappeared now, and the fags vanished from the house soon after. I must have passed the point where I had taken it up.

Not going in to work gave me time to plan how I was going to prevent Sarah's death. It also allowed me to spend time with a grieving Stacey who had grown progressively unhappy as the year had regressed. She no longer had David in her life to support her; they had met at Christmas 2018, so she was now alone, away at university and grieving over the loss of her mother. Just as I had grown younger, so had she, and far from being the confident young woman I had first known, she now seemed barely more than a child taking her first steps into the adult world.

She had only been at university for one term when her mother died, and she had not been able to face going back for the next one. She had eventually returned in February, and I knew that I faced a January full of tears and heartbreak.

To have her mother ripped away from her so suddenly and cruelly had completely devastated her world. I comforted her as best I could, but there was nothing I could do until the fateful day arrived. The hurt and pain she was suffering built up anger within myself, and I was determined that I was going to stop the man who had caused it, no matter how far I had to go.

I knew everything I needed to know about him. His name was Mark Tompkins; he was 34 years old and lived on an estate in East Oxford. All the details had come out during the trial, after which he had been sentenced to fourteen years in prison for causing death by dangerous driving. Although that was the maximum the law allowed, it still wasn't enough in my opinion.

Ironically, despite the hatred I felt towards the man, what I was planning to do was going to save him from that prison sentence. It wasn't just enough to make sure that Sarah wasn't on the zebra crossing to be mown down at the appointed place and time. If I did that, there was nothing to prevent him carrying on his drink-driving and killing some other poor family's mother, father or child. He needed to be stopped.

How far could I go? Some dark thoughts clouded my mind. What would happen if I killed him during the day of the accident? No one would have any reason to suspect me. If I killed him before he killed Sarah, there would be no possible connection. She would live, and he wouldn't be able to stagger drunk into his car ever again.

Ultimately, I dismissed this thought. I couldn't really see myself killing someone in cold blood. Instead I worked out a plan that would resolve everything to my satisfaction and got it ready to put into operation. Before any of that could happen, though, there was the funeral and Christmas to get through.

**December 2017**

Christmas 2017 was an awful, miserable time in our house. Sarah had been killed on the night of the 22nd, so close to the big day that the house was already decked out for the occasion. The turkey was in the fridge and the tree was decorated, with presents wrapped and laid out beneath it. Sarah's were destined never to be opened. The day had been spent wallowing in grief and self-pity. Although I knew that all of this was going to be put right, I couldn't cope with the sheer emotion of the situation, in particular Stacey's anguish: so traumatic that I found myself also breaking down and sobbing. I thought the funeral which had taken place five days later had been bad enough, but nothing could compare to that awful Christmas Day.

Somehow we got through it, and then there was one further day of suffering on Christmas Eve. After that came the 23rd, the day after Sarah's death, when I had been steeling myself for more of the same, but as it happened, things turned out differently to how I had been expecting.

I woke up alone in bed on what was to be my last day as a widower. I went downstairs to the kitchen where Stacey was already making breakfast. Two pieces of bread popped up from the toaster as I entered the room, and she keenly turned round to me and said, "Hi, Dad, where's Mum?"

I had become pretty good at anticipating things that might happen on a daily basis, but it hadn't crossed my mind to think that she might not be aware yet of her mother's death. "Oh, she had to go out early," I said, thinking on the spot as I so often had to in my crazy life. "A bit of last-minute Christmas shopping, I think."

"Cool," replied Stacey, as she grabbed a knife from the drawer and began to spread some butter on her toast. "I still need to do a bit myself," she added.

I hadn't seen her like this for months. She was quite her old self, a bubbly, cheerful eighteen-year-old girl looking forward to Christmas. At that moment, I made a snap decision. I had absolutely no need to tell her of her mother's death. I couldn't bear the thought of inflicting that misery and pain on her. There had been more than enough of that over the past few weeks to last a lifetime. I had made up my mind. We were getting out of the city for the day.

"As it happens, I still need to do a bit, too," I said. "In fact, as it's the weekend, and Mum's going to be busy getting everything ready for Christmas, why don't you and I go shopping together? It'll be fun."

"I'd love that!" said Stacey. "You haven't taken me shopping for years. It'll be like when I was little and you used to push me around in the trolley."

"Apart from the fact that I don't think you'll fit in there anymore," I joked. "Tell you what, let's make a real day of it and go to London."

"Fantastic," replied Stacey. "Do you think Mum will want to come?"

"She's going to be too busy today," I replied. "She won't mind us going. I'll text her and let her know."

I had to make sure that no one could get in touch with Stacey. The last thing I wanted was someone contacting her with a text message along the lines of *"Sorry to hear about your mum"*. So, while she was upstairs getting ready, I took her mobile out of her handbag and hid it down the side of the sofa.

I hurried Stacey out of the house as quickly as I could and down to Oxford railway station where we caught a train to Paddington. Once we were in London, we shopped like there was no tomorrow at Harrods, Selfridges and Fortnum & Mason. By the time we'd finished, it was already getting dark and it was time to put phase two of the operation into place.

"Shouldn't we be getting back?" asked Stacey. "Mum will be wondering where we are. I wish I had my phone. I'm sure I put it in my bag before we left."

"Yeah, bad news on that front, I'm afraid," I said. "Mum texted me earlier – apparently all the train drivers have walked out on strike in a dispute over Christmas pay. We can't get home by train today." It was a pretty lame excuse, but she bought it and, since she had no phone, she couldn't check the news to discover that I'd made it up.

"What about the buses?" asked Stacey.

"Let's forget the buses," I said. "I'm in one of the most famous cities in the world with one of my two favourite people in the world. Let's stay over and make a night of it."

Stacey was thrilled. She had been to London before, as she'd already mentioned earlier in the day about the time I'd taken her to the Aquarium and the Science Museum a few years ago. This was her first time as an adult. Of course, I already knew London very well from my gambling-funded exploits, so I booked us a couple of rooms at one of my favourite hotels. Last time I'd stayed in this hotel it had been with one of London's finest hookers at £800 an hour for the pleasure. All of that was long behind me now. Being with Stacey, enjoying some family time, was infinitely preferable.

We dined at a lovely little steakhouse in Covent Garden, washing down our meal with plenty of drinks. I was certainly splashing the cash about. Unlike before when it had come out of the bookies' satchels, this time it was all going on the corporate Amex. Plenty of other colleagues did it and just claimed it as "entertaining clients", some getting into trouble for it, but I didn't have any of that to worry about. It fell neatly into the box marked "No consequences".

I'd definitely done the right thing. Stacey had really enjoyed her day and I had got to spend some quality time with her. I had successfully shielded her from the news of her mother's death and pretty soon, if all went according to plan, she would never have died in the first place.

The following morning I awoke back at home. This had been the day that I had been looking forward to more than any other since my life had begun. I was not to be disappointed. I opened my eyes, and there, lying on her side, back turned to me was my beautiful, resurrected wife, sleeping peacefully.

I sat up and took a while just to look at her. Her long, blonde hair reminded me very much of how Stacey's had looked when I had first seen her. Her naked body was slender with smooth, pale skin unblemished by the passing of time. She looked much younger, at 39 years old, than I had expected she would.

I lay back down, pulled the covers over and snuggled into her, touching her body for the first time. I had wondered for so long what this moment would be like, and now that she was here, it seemed almost unreal.

I put my arm around her, and she awoke, turning to me and giving me the chance to see her face properly for the first time. I'd seen her in photos a thousand times, but they didn't do her justice. She really was beautiful. There was no doubting where Stacey had got her looks from.

Excited to be close to her naked flesh, I felt some familiar stirrings down below. She felt them, too, pressing into her leg and, amused, she said, "To what do I owe this pleasure? It's not my birthday, is it?"

I had never heard her voice before, and it came as a surprise. I knew she had been born and bred in South Wales, but the accent still caught me unawares. I liked it, though: she had a lovely, lilting, tone that instantly attracted me, as if I wasn't turned on enough already.

"No, it's not your birthday," I replied, "but it is the first day of the rest of your life," and, unable to contain myself any longer, I slipped my hand down between her legs and let nature take its course.

Such was my state of excitement that it was all over very quickly, something Sarah wasn't shy about remarking upon.

"That was quick," she said. "Not like you at all. I trust you're going to help me finish myself off?" And with that she reached into her bedside table and pulled out a monstrous-looking device I'd later discover was known as a Rabbit.

"My pleasure," I said, getting to grips with the toy. "You know perhaps we should do it more often," I suggested. "It might slow me down a bit."

"You'll get no complaints from me on that front," she said, sighing, as I got busy with the toy.

This was a most promising start to married life. My gorgeous, sexy wife was clearly no prude, and all of this was in stark contrast to the bleak picture that Nick had painted of his two failed marriages. He was of the opinion that sex died completely after ten years with someone. Well, that might have been true in his case and this morning's session may have had some novelty value for me, but Sarah didn't seem like someone who'd lost any enthusiasm for sex and we had been married for eighteen years.

I wasn't planning on going into work on this most important of days, so I phoned the office and made up some story about driving to Norfolk to negotiate a new contract with a company that made bog cleaner. One of the great things about being the boss was that no one ever questioned me. Sarah was definitely going to work, though, and there was no point me trying to talk her out of it. She worked in a small legal firm, and today was the day of their Christmas party.

"Don't forget I won't be home tonight," she said, over breakfast. "We're going straight into town for our Christmas do after work. Probably won't be back until pretty late."

"That's OK," I said, then added, "I'll wait up for you."

"I'll probably be pretty hammered when I get back," she added, "if last year is anything to go by."

After she went, I kissed her goodbye and made my preparations for the day. The words "I won't be home tonight" echoed in my mind, thinking about how she hadn't come home ever again. But today that would all change. This time it was going to be different.

I knew exactly where and when the accident had taken place, and where to find Tompkins during the evening. This was further evidence that had come out at the trial, but to make sure, I had tracked him down already to ensure there would be no case of mistaken identity.

The information I had was that he had driven his car to a pub a couple of miles from Oxford city centre and had parked it in their car park at around teatime that afternoon. I hadn't seen the car before: for whatever reason it hadn't been parked at his house when I went to check him out, but I knew what I was looking for.

I drove to the car park myself and sat in my car and waited. It was dark by the time he arrived, around 4.30pm, but I still spotted the car instantly under the street lights, a beaten-up old red Nova with a 1993 registration plate.

He parked in a space almost directly opposite me, got out and headed into the pub. I decided to follow. I wanted to find out for myself what my wife's killer was like.

At his trial he'd painted a picture of a family man who'd made a single terrible mistake. I knew that he was married with two kids, so if he really was the family man he claimed, why would he be driving to the pub at this time on a Friday afternoon? Surely most fathers would be looking forward to spending some time with their kids at the end of the working week, wouldn't they?

It wasn't as if he was even attending a work Christmas party: he just seemed to be on his own, at least at first. I walked into the pub, ordered myself a soft drink and watched to see what he did. It was busy in the pub, full of people who had just finished work for the Christmas break, and the place was full of festive cheer.

After about ten minutes he was already three-quarters of the way down his first pint of lager, having been standing playing a fruit machine on his own. Cash exhausted, he thumped the buttons on the front of the machine, swore at it, and headed across to a pool table in the corner where a group of young men were playing. He chalked his name up on a blackboard which read "Winner stays on" and started joining in the banter with the others.

By 8pm, he was on his fifth pint and it was still over three hours until the fateful moment of the accident. It was time for me to head out into the car park and put the next part of my plan into operation.

It was my intention to phone the police and report him for drinking and driving, but I couldn't be sure that it would be enough to stop him. What if the police didn't come? It was one of their busiest nights of the year after all, commonly known as "Mad Friday". Town would be full of people who didn't normally drink, overdoing it and getting out of control. The increasingly cash-strapped police forces were going to find their resources highly stretched tonight. So for good measure, I went and let down one of his tyres, the nearside rear. Hopefully he wouldn't notice and would still get in the car. I would need him to do this if the police were to be able to arrest him. A flat tyre would also delay him from getting away, giving Sarah ample time to make it over the zebra crossing safely.

Had I done enough, though? What if the police didn't come and he decided to change the wheel and drive off? He might end up killing someone else. I couldn't imagine he'd be up to changing a wheel in his inebriated state, but anything was possible. What if he decided not to drive home and left the car behind? That would solve the problem for tonight, but what about in the future? It was all very noble of me, saving Sarah's life, but if he got away scot-free I'd only be saving up his lethal combination of booze and car for another night.

Worst of all, he might be so drunk he wouldn't even notice the tyre was flat, turning the car into an even more lethal weapon than it already was. I had a plan C in mind if neither the police nor the flat tyre stopped him, but it was very much a last resort. I needed him to get caught by the police one way or another, as the man had to be punished for the crime he was yet to commit.

The timing of my call was crucial. The accident had occurred at 11.22pm. If I rang the police too early they would get here, find that he was still in the pub and leave again, as no crime had been committed. Too late, and he would already have left. It was reminiscent of the time that I'd deliberated about what time to call the fire brigade about the fire at the furniture store. Timing was crucial. I decided I would make the call at precisely 11pm.

The time seemed to crawl by as I sat in my car. At half past ten I decided to go back into the pub and find out what was happening. It was absolutely packed and very noisy. A fat, middle-aged man in an Animal T-shirt was running a disco in the corner and the music was deafening. It took some time to fight my way through to the other end of the pub where the pool table was. Tompkins was still there, and engaged in a heated argument with another man over whose turn it was next. As I watched, he brandished the pool cue at the man who wisely backed down.

I had no idea how much he'd had to drink but he was swaying and slopping his pint all over the place. I'd seen enough. All those crocodile tears I'd seen him put on at his trial were an absolute farce. The man was a drunk and a bully. "Family man, my arse," I muttered to myself as I turned and headed back for the car park. Well, he was just about to get his come-uppance.

It was nearly 11pm when I got back to the car, so I dialled 999 and asked to be put through to the police. It took some time to get all the details through, at which point I got chastised for calling the emergency number rather than 101.

"But this is an emergency," I exclaimed. "This bloke in the pub is extremely drunk and aggressive, and he told me himself he was going to drive home, boasting that he'd never been caught. His exact words were "Bollocks to the pigs", if I recall correctly."

OK, so I had made the last bit up for dramatic effect, but I still wasn't getting the response I wanted. Eventually, the lady on the other end of the line agreed to send someone out, but I wasn't convinced, and the conversation had taken so long, there wasn't much time to spare. I should have phoned earlier.

I sat back in the car and waited. As expected, at a quarter past eleven he came staggering out through the back gate towards his car. He was clearly angry, shouting and swearing.

"Fucking wankers!" he shouted, looking back towards the pub, before tripping over an empty yellow beer crate that had been left just outside the gate. Just managing to stay on his feet, he crossed over to his car, fumbled in his jacket pocket for his keys and promptly dropped them on the ground. Frustratingly there was no sign whatsoever of the police.

He got into his car, switched on the ignition and began to pull out of the space, seemingly unaware that he had a flat. There was nothing else for it. I was going to have to resort to plan C. I turned on the ignition, engaged first gear and slammed down the accelerator. Holding my breath and praying the air bag would deploy, I closed my eyes and braced for the impact.

It was far more of a shock than I had expected. Our two cars had been parked barely ten yards apart, but the crash was significant. The sound of breaking glass was everywhere. My air bag did indeed go off in my face which wasn't particularly pleasant but that, along with the seat belt, almost certainly saved me from any serious injury. In fact, other than a slight pain in the back of my neck which I attributed to whiplash, I felt OK physically. Emotionally, I was a wreck, heart thumping away at such a rate of knots I feared for a moment I was going to have a heart attack.

The sound of the crash had brought drinkers running from the pub garden. "Call an ambulance," I heard a girl's voice shout. "And get the police," called another. "It's that twat who started the fight over the pool table. There's no way he should have been driving, he's had a right skinful."

"Are you alright, mate?" said a young man, no older than his early twenties, as he opened my driver's side door.

"I'm OK," I said, "just a little bit of whiplash," I said, as he helped me out of the car.

"He wasn't so lucky," replied the young man, gesturing at the other car. I looked to see that Tompkins had hit his head on the windscreen. Not only did his old car not have an air bag, he also hadn't been wearing his seat belt. Serves the arsehole right, I thought.

"Is he dead?" I asked, half-hoping that he was. That would be poetic justice. And with him drunk, and me sober, there would be no doubt who would be blamed.

"I don't think so," said the man. "You weren't going fast enough. He's in a pretty bad way, though. That's what happens when you drink and drive."

A minute or two later, I heard the sirens of the approaching ambulance and police cars. It was a shame that an accident had to have taken place before they'd come out; had they heeded my earlier warnings, none of this needed to have happened.

Tompkins was indeed not dead, but unconscious and pretty badly smashed up. I didn't feel any remorse. I hadn't intended to injure him so badly, just prevent him from hurting anybody else. I was confident that once the police had investigated fully, they would conclude that I was blameless. I hadn't touched a drop of alcohol that day as they soon discovered, breathalysing me at the scene as a matter of routine. Once they'd heard from others in the pub about Tompkins' drunken behaviour, they were sure to get his blood tested at the hospital. He'd wake up to discover himself with a smashed up face and severely in the shit with the police. All in all, it was a job well done.

The police wanted to interview me at the scene, but first I needed to make sure that Sarah was OK. Although I'd had plenty of experience of altering the future before, there remained a nagging doubt in my mind. I feared that somehow something else might happen to her to "protect the timeline", as I'd recently seen happen in an old movie about some teenagers cheating death. It was nearly a quarter to twelve by now, and I was incredibly relieved when she answered the phone to reveal that she was in a taxi on the way home.

I explained to her that I'd been in a car accident and that I was perfectly alright, but she insisted on getting the taxi to turn around and bring her directly to me. I wasn't going to complain. Until I could physically see she was safe, I wouldn't be happy.

I was talking to the police ten minutes later when she arrived in the taxi and flung her arms around me. I felt hugely reassured by this and knew that, for now at least, the world had been put to rights.

# Stacey

**August 2017**

Sarah's arrival in my life had changed it beyond all recognition. Whatever sparkle had initially brought us together was still there, and I swiftly found myself falling in love with her.

We were soulmates, best friends and constant companions. My past debauched behaviour was soon forgotten as I slipped quickly and easily into the relationship. There never seemed to be any shortage of things to talk about, we simply gelled and that was all there was to it.

Throughout 2018 I had noticed the weight falling off me, and once I was back with Sarah I began to notice further changes, not only in my appearance, but also in how I felt. Being with her meant I ate much more healthily than I had after her death when I'd really let myself go. My skin looked better, my hangovers were gone, and so were all the niggling aches and pains. My clothes had gone from XL to L to M and I felt good in them.

It wasn't all down to healthier living. Many of the changes were down to the physical properties of my ever younger body. The grey continued to disappear from my hair. It had almost completely covered the bald patch by now, leaving me with a full head of thick, black hair. My teeth were much improved, as was my eyesight. By the time of my 46$^{th}$ birthday in 2016, I was able to begin managing without my glasses. Which was just as well, really, as soon after that, they vanished.

My social life also took off after Sarah's return. Suddenly we were attending weddings and parties, and meeting other friends at weekends. Sarah was a very active person and for every evening we sat contentedly at home watching TV together, there would be another when she was out at a class or at the gym. I, too, discovered that I had a sporting side when I began playing squash with Nick on Thursday evenings, a sport at which I was pleasantly surprised to discover I excelled.

I was still crap at golf, though. In addition to the annual charity do, I was also part of a society that went out four times a year. Whatever course we attended, it was the same woeful display, and the club shops must have done pretty well out of me when they went to dredge the lakes for balls. I quite enjoyed the days out with the golf society, and was glad I hadn't kept to my resolution to avoid golf at all costs.

Another enjoyable addition to my married life was the taking of holidays. My trips abroad to date had consistently entirely of business travel. It seemed I hadn't bothered with holidays in my widower years, so I was pleased to discover that I had plenty of holidays to look forward to. The excitement tended to build backwards as the holiday approached, and I usually got a good idea of what to expect from the hundreds of pictures Sarah always insisted on loading up to Facebook.

The only downside of holidays was the travelling. Going home on the last day wasn't so bad, as I'd still have the holiday to look forward to, but the first day of the holiday was always a real chore. It seemed pointless going through all the hassle of flying out to somewhere when I knew I'd only end up back home the next day. But I'd resolved to try and live as normally as possible, which included not letting on to Sarah about my trek back through time, so I just went along with it. It was less hassle to go through with the journey than having to come up with explanations as to why I wasn't going, not to mention disappointing Sarah and Stacey.

Most people checked the weather forecast to see what the weather was going to be like on holiday, whereas I just looked up past statistics. They were much more accurate than weather forecasts. I also got a good idea of how much sun I was going to get just by looking at my skin. In the run-up to two weeks in Crete in August 2017 I turned a rich shade of golden brown, so the weather must have been good. When I awoke there on the first morning, I wasn't disappointed. Flinging open the shutters on the windows of our villa, I was greeted with the gorgeous sight of the sun's rays shining down upon a sparkling blue Aegean sea.

Such was the laid-back lifestyle of those two blissful weeks in that sleepy part of the Western Crete coast that I was able to forget about my backwards spiral through time and just enjoy the days as they came. We mixed lazy days at the beach with sightseeing, and in the evening spent long hours in tavernas, eating and drinking. One day was much like another, and I relished being able to spend my days with Sarah, just the two of us in the most idyllic place I had ever been.

Apparently this was the first holiday that we'd had without Stacey since she had been born. She was eighteen now, and had decided to go on a girls' holiday to Majorca with two of her school friends, Sophie and Amelia, to celebrate finishing their A Levels.

It was during that holiday in Crete that I became further aware of the dark clouds hanging over Stacey's past. One night when we were in a taverna, Sarah expressed concern about her being out in Majorca with her friends at such a tender age.

"I do wonder if we did the right thing, letting her go out there," said Sarah.

"We have to cut the apron strings eventually," I replied. "She's eighteen now, she has to be allowed to spread her wings." I was able to speak with some confidence, having seen the well-rounded, mature person that Stacey had become in her twenties.

"I know," replied Sarah. "But I can't bear the thought that something might happen to her again like before. After all we've been through over the last couple of years with her, something like that could completely destroy her."

I knew that no harm had come to Stacey in Majorca, so I could try and reassure Sarah on that score, but what had happened before? How could I ask? Or should I bide my time and wait for it to come out.

"I'm sure she will be fine," I said. "You said yourself that the girls had promised to stick together."

"I think I'll ring her, just to make sure," replied Sarah, reaching into her bag for her mobile.

All was well with the phone call and I decided not to pursue the matter further. If this was the only holiday Sarah and I were to have alone, I didn't want to spoil even one day by discussing less happy times. I would find out what I needed to in the fullness of time.

### March 2016

It was not until we were on holiday in Florida the following year that I was to find out exactly what had happened to Stacey. I knew that it must have been something very bad, but even I wasn't prepared for the truth of what had happened the previous summer.

It was the first time I had been to America. Despite my many travels around Europe with the company, I hadn't been any further afield; we were strictly a European operation. So this was the first time I had moved significantly outside my time zone, which threw up an interesting anomaly.

I had long ago realised that my 3am time jump was fixed at that time throughout the year and altered along with the clocks. So during the summer months when Greenwich Mean Time was replaced by British Summer Time, my jump would change to 4am. The vast majority of the time I didn't notice, but when I arrived in Florida, I certainly did.

The clocks hadn't gone forward yet in the UK so I was still jumping back at 3am at home. It had slipped my mind to consider the time difference, so I was taken completely unawares what happened on the day I arrived. On the last day, rather than waking up in a hotel room as I was expecting, I found myself materialising fully awake in the middle of a restaurant somewhere in the Tampa Bay area. I was sitting at a table for three with Sarah and Stacey. A young waitress was standing over us, mid-order.

"What about you, Dad?" asked Stacey.

"Uh, yeah," I mumbled, bluffing as I frequently had to. "I'll have the same."

"So that's three hot fudge sundaes, then," said Sarah. "That's not like you. You normally ask for an Irish coffee."

"Oh, yes, I'll have one of those, too," I quickly added.

"Greedy!" said Sarah. "You'll be putting on weight."

"Well, I am on holiday," I replied.

The five hour difference meant that for the first time in my life, I actually had the novelty of going to bed that night and waking up on the actual next day. I then had to go through the usual hassle of flying all the way back to the UK before I could start my holiday properly. After that it was fun all the way. In the daytime we visited the best theme parks Florida had to offer, and in the evening we had the most gorgeous and very generously portioned meals. The steaks were fantastic, bigger and better than anything I'd had back home. I made sure we dined as early as possible. The last thing I wanted to do was to be just starting to tuck into a nice juicy steak, only to vanish back in time to the previous day.

One day I managed to get us to Tampa Bay Races to enjoy some horse racing US style. With the previous days' racing results committed to memory, we were able to pull off some spectacular long odds bets on the exotic wagering available at the track. Exactas, Trifectas and even Superfectas (selecting the first four horses in correct order) were easy pickings, and we ate and drank extremely well that night.

Around midway through the holidays I finally got the chance to find out what had been nagging at my mind for so long: the truth about what had happened to Stacey.

It was late at night and Sarah and I were talking in bed after getting intimate. Cuddled up in the afterglow, she said, "You know I'm so glad we brought Stacey out here. It's the first time I've seen her really happy since what happened last summer."

Seizing my opportunity, I asked, "Do you think there's anything we could have done to make things turn out differently?"

It was a bit of a vague question, but it got Sarah to open up. "I really don't know," she said. "How could we have known? I've been over it in my mind a thousand times."

"Let's go over it again," I said.

"Must we?" she asked. "We're having such a nice time on this holiday. I really don't want to drag it all up again. Please, can't we just forget about it?"

"Just this once," I said, adding, "I need closure", which was a bullshit phrase I'd heard on some soap opera that seemed to fit the moment. "Then I promise we'll never mention it again."

And so, Sarah opened up and we went over the details, me carefully asking her leading questions to get the whole story without it being too obvious I knew nothing about it.

By the end of the conversation, I knew it all. I was horrified, distressed and angry in equal measures. What had been done to my little girl was enough to make me want blood. I'm sure any father would have felt the same.

In July 2015, Stacey's school had thrown an end-of-term prom for the Year 11 students in celebration of them finishing their GCSEs. During the evening, Stacey had been the subject of some over-amorous attentions from one of the boys in her class. Liam was the captain of the school football team, popular, good-looking and with no shortage of female attention. Unknown to Stacey at the time, he had already slept with four girls in her year, and had openly bragged that he planned to shag them all. She knew none of this so was delighted when he asked her to be his date for the prom.

Stacey was flattered by his attentions, but she was still a virgin at the time and not ready for any sort of sexual relationship. Late in the evening, he'd suggested taking a walk onto the school field. Naively perhaps, she had followed, expecting a little kissing but nothing more.

Unfortunately, Liam was used to getting what he wanted, and he was expecting a lot more than she was willing to give. When Stacey had resisted, he had raped her behind the cricket pavilion.

She had been so traumatised by the event that she had gone straight home and washed away the evidence, telling no one what had happened. She had been miserable and withdrawn for weeks, but refused to say what was wrong, even to her mother.

Eventually, in September, she'd turned to Sarah in tears after discovering she was pregnant. The two of them had hidden it from me initially, but it all came out after she had an abortion and I had forced it out of Sarah, knowing something was clearly wrong.

Apparently I had wanted to go and kill the bloke, but had been dissuaded by Sarah. Then we had tried to persuade Stacey to go to the police, but she had refused. She couldn't face going through the whole interview process or a lengthy court case. So it seemed Liam had got away with it.

But he had reckoned without me, the time-travelling avenger, heading back to right another wrong perpetrated against my family. And this time, I was going to make certain he would never dare lay a finger on another woman against her will ever again.

**July 2015**

The day of the prom had arrived, and I had my plans all worked out. Just as I had with Tompkins, I'd had months to track down Liam and suss him out. I didn't like what I'd seen.

I stalked him on the internet, and tracked him down in real life. I followed him around Oxford, watching what he did. Hanging out with his mates, he liked to play the big "I am", bragging about his sexual conquests and how great he was at football. He claimed that he was having trials with a Premiership football club and was going to earn £250k a week and shag whoever he liked. He was arrogant, egotistical and rude. As far as he was concerned, he was God's gift to women, and they were his for the taking. He showed no signs of any remorse at all for what he'd done to Stacey.

It made me so angry it was all I could do to stop myself killing him there and then. Sitting in the bath one evening I fantasised about all the ways I could bring him down. The beauty of it was, if I really wanted to I could kill him as many times as I wanted. He'd be back again the next day and I could do it all over again. I could push him under a bus on Sunday and then slit his throat on Saturday. As I lay back and relaxed under the bubbles, I devised all manner of grisly and evil plans.

Of course, I had no intention of actually carrying out any of these plans, but I'm sure most people have had such thoughts in their darker moments. I'd done so much good work up to this point to change my future timeline there was no point undoing it all again by risking spending the rest of my life in prison. So I decided to bide my time and wait for the day of the event itself. Then he would be in for a shock.

On the day of the prom, Stacey looked stunning. Sixteen years old, dressed in a pink, 1950s-style prom dress, she was set to be the belle of the ball.

She had chosen her outfit to fit in with the school's 1950s *Grease* theme. When Liam turned up to collect Stacey he was wearing one of those classic varsity-style jackets that frat boys always donned in old American teen movies, red with white sleeves and a large letter "D" on the front.

He was polite enough at the door, addressing me as "Mr Scott", though I couldn't help but notice the insincerity in his voice. Through gritted teeth I forced myself to respond nicely, even though every bone in my body wanted to punch his lights out.

Some might have questioned what on earth I was doing letting her go off with him, knowing what I knew, but I had to let things play out as they had done before. Nothing bad was going to happen until he took her down to the field, and then I would put my plan into action.

I could have simply stopped Stacey from going to the ball, but all that would have achieved would have been to make her angry and resentful with me, and it wouldn't have put a stop to his ways. She seemed to think he was the bee's knees, the way she was talking about him all through the day of the prom. I needed her to see exactly what he was really like before I intervened.

The school was on the banks of the River Cherwell, with a school field that was accessible over a small bridge. The entrance was not locked so I waited until dusk fell and then crept in under cover of darkness. It was vital no one saw me because Liam was going to be in a sorry state by the time I'd finished with him, and I did not want any witnesses placing me at the scene.

By 10pm, I had secreted myself by the side of the pavilion behind an old water tank which provided perfect cover. I had about an hour or so to wait which gave me time for some final reflections on how I was going to handle this. How far should I let things go? If I was to intervene too early, Stacey wouldn't thank me for it; too late and she'd be seriously traumatised. I had no choice but to play it by ear and see what happened.

It was a warm, moonlit night, and the air was still. Watching from behind the tank I saw them approaching, hand-in-hand, across the bridge. The still air meant that their voices carried easily and I could hear the conversation from some way off. As they grew closer, I crouched down a little further to ensure I wouldn't be spotted.

Stacey sounded happy at this stage: they were laughing and joking together. He seemed to be acting like the perfect gentleman, but I knew it was a façade. At least I hoped it was. An unwelcome element of doubt had crept into my mind. What if she had made the whole thing up? That he hadn't raped her at all, but she'd said he had because she was so ashamed of the pregnancy? There had been a similar high-profile case in the news in 2018 involving a well-known popstar and an obsessed fan. His name had been blackened all over the tabloids, until she finally admitted she'd fabricated the whole story in revenge for him rejecting her. Mud stuck, though, and his career never recovered.

I swiftly dismissed these unworthy thoughts. It was not the sort of thing Stacey would do. She had never lied to me and I knew from the state she'd been in over the past few months that this was no fake rape.

Sure enough, as they stopped behind the pavilion on the short strip of grass separating it from the river bank, things began to get heated. They were barely ten yards from my position, so I was very cautious as I risked a look from behind the tank to see what was happening.

They were kissing deeply, and as I watched I saw him move his hand to her breast. As he did so, she firmly moved it away. He tried again, more forcefully, and this time she broke the kiss, and clearly said, "No."

He had been all charm and humour up to that point, but this was the trigger point for his Jekyll and Hyde moment. "Come on, you know you want it," he said loudly, pushing her back against the wall of the pavilion and forcing his mouth upon hers once more.

"No I don't," she proclaimed gutsily. Good for her, I thought, at least she's standing up for herself.

"That's not what I came out here for," she added.

"Well what did you think we came out here for?" he shouted angrily. "To kiss and hold hands? This is the 21st century, not *Downton Abbey*. Now stop fucking me around and get your knickers off." And with that he grabbed hold of her again, and roughly tried to shove his hand up her dress and between her legs.

"Get off me," she screamed, as he pushed her to the ground and forced himself on top of her.

"Shut the fuck up, you stupid bitch, and just enjoy it. Your mate Sophie did," he shouted. He tore at her dress which gave way with an audible rip. She screamed. I had let things go far enough. It was time to intervene.

I leapt up from behind the water tank, and sprinted over to them, shouting "Get the fuck off of her." Startled by my unexpected apparition, he attempted to get up but I had already reached them. I cannoned straight into him, sending him sprawling backwards towards the river bank. As I watched him topple backwards almost in slow motion, Stacey was screaming hysterically behind me.

It hadn't been my intention to push him into the river. What I had planned to do was to kick the living shit out of him, but now, as I watched, things took an unexpected turn. He fell directly backwards into the water with a huge splash, right into a dense patch of reeds.

I had expected him to climb straight back out, but he didn't. The shock of hitting the water must have taken his breath away, and he'd gone completely under. The reeds were very thick, and he appeared to have been caught up in them.

He was almost completely immersed, his hands grasping desperately above the water as he thrashed about, but it was all over very quickly. Suddenly he was very silent and very still. I had heard stories of people drowning in a few inches of water, but I really hadn't expected him to succumb this easily. Perhaps he'd hit his head when he'd fallen in.

I certainly wasn't going to any effort to fish him out. The bastard had got what he'd deserved as far as I was concerned. All these months I'd been fantasising about ways to do him in, and now I'd accomplished it without even intending to. Now I had a situation to deal with.

My first thought was for Stacey, distraught and hysterical. I turned back towards her, dress torn, make-up running with tears, and hair a dishevelled mess. Quickly, I gathered her up in my arms as she sobbed her heart out. After what seemed an age, but was in fact probably only about fifteen seconds, she spoke.

"Is he dead?" she asked.

"I think so," I replied.

"Oh my God," she said, and began crying again.

"I didn't mean to kill him," I said. "You have to believe me, Stacey. He was going to rape you. I was just trying to get him off you."

"I know," she said. "It was horrible. I had no idea he would be like that. But how did you know? How did you come to be here?"

I had been prepared for these questions.

"I found out tonight," I said. "I went out for a drink with a couple of the guys I play golf with and I told them about the prom. One of them told me he knew Liam, and that he'd tried to force himself upon his daughter last year. He suggested I come down here and check you were OK. So, I hurried here as quickly as I could. When I got to the gates, I saw you walking down here and followed. Looks like I got here just in time."

It was complete bullshit, but she bought it.

"I'm glad you did. I'm sorry, Dad, I shouldn't have let him talk me into coming down here," she said, and burst into tears again.

"It's what we do now, that's important," I said. I needed to come up with a revised plan to take into account the new circumstances. There was a world of difference between a beaten-up body and a dead one face-down in the water. Stacey was still sobbing, but I needed her to be strong as I began to outline my plan to her.

"The first thing you need to do is to ring my mobile, and we need to have a conversation. You tell me you've been attacked, where you are, and that he's fallen into the river. You are panicking and you don't know what to do. I will tell you to ring the police and that I will be right there. It's vital we do this, as when the police investigate they will check our mobile phone records. I've turned all the GPS and other tracking stuff off from my phone, so they won't exactly know where I was when you made the call."

Stacey nodded her understanding. I continued.

"Then give it five minutes and call the police. Don't leave it any longer than that or they will question why it took so long for you to call after you had spoken to me. When they get here, I'll claim to have got here a couple of minutes before them. All you need to do then is tell them he attacked you and that you fought him off and he fell into the river. It's vital we make sure this looks like an accident. Neither of us wants to be under any suspicion here."

Stacey pulled herself together and did as she was told. I then held her close to me as we waited for the police to arrive. I had no regrets over what had happened. Stacey was safe and there was one less arsehole in the world.

I just hoped she would still look at me in the same light in the future and not see her dad as a killer. I didn't think she would: I had been defending her, after all. He'd been attacking her, I had pushed him off, and he had fallen into the river.

The police came, along with forensics and did their stuff. They were sympathetic towards Stacey and eventually allowed us both to go home, saying that they would need to see us the next day for statements.

If there were to be any repercussions, I had no way of finding out, I just had to hope I had done enough to convince them. A coroner's verdict of accident or misadventure was what I was hoping for, leaving us all in the clear.

With Stacey still upset and traumatised, I accepted the offer of a lift home in a police car. When we got through the front door, she fell into her mother's arms and wept, causing me to well up too, in relief, if nothing else, that it was all over. The three of us were safe, together and at home. We were alive and well, with the triple whammy of rape, death by dangerous driving and cancer hopefully vanquished from our lives forever.

All I wanted now was my family. Forwards or backwards, Sarah and Stacey were my life, and nothing else mattered.

# London

**December 2010**

Almost five years had passed since the night I'd rescued Stacey from Liam's clutches, sending him to a watery grave. Since then, I'd finally been able to relax and get on with trying to lead as normal a life as possible.

Landmark events did, of course, come along from time to time, and the next major change I needed to prepare myself for was the arrival of my parents in my life.

It was a bitterly cold Friday afternoon about a week before Christmas as I stood with assorted mourners saying goodbye to my dead mother.

After the service, we walked up through the garden of remembrance to look at the flowers. Stacey was crying, just eleven years old now, and she gripped my gloved hand tightly. There was snow in the air. The following morning I had woken up to the deepest snowfall I had ever seen, for once giving the Christmas season a festive feel.

It seemed that death haunted my family around Christmas time. Both my mother and wife had died in the run-up to Christmas, not to mention my own death on New Year's Day. Mum had been 70 years of age when she'd died suddenly in her sleep the previous week.

After careful consideration, I had decided I was not going to do anything about it. She had lived a good life and had a peaceful death which is all any of us can hope for. I saw no point in trying to prevent the heart attack that had claimed her, only for her to likely succumb to it soon after, anyway. It would either be that or she would face a painful old age, dosed up with medication to try and stave off the inevitable. It just seemed the best thing to do to let her go.

I was looking forward to getting to know her so I made sure that on the day before she died I went to visit. She didn't seem unwell in any way, and was pleasantly surprised to see the three of us roll up that Sunday morning at her home in Botley and offer to take her out to lunch.

My mother was a rich source of information about the past, and had no reluctance at all about imparting it. She was at that age where she was looking back at a life well-led, reminiscing about all the good times and various family members. I learnt more about my family history that one lunchtime than I'd accumulated in the whole of the previous fourteen years.

She was a wartime baby, just like my father, and they had met when she'd been working as a cashier in a betting shop in the 1960s. My dad used to punt there regularly, and when he got three winners up in a patent one Saturday, he'd asked her if she fancied a night out on the winnings. The rest was history, married in 1968, and then I came along in 1970. So now, not only did I know how I'd come to be in the world, I also knew where my love of horse racing and gambling had come from.

My mother's death in December 2010 coincided with my promotion to Marketing Director at work. My upgrade in status meant that I got a brand new top-of-the-range BMW to replace my old car, but getting hold of the keys on the day it arrived proved problematical. Barry had been given the task of handing them over to me, and when I went down to the security desk, he refused.

"I've heard my new car is here," I said, trying to sound excited, even though I'd been driving it for the past two years. "Can I have the keys please?"

"No," replied Barry, bluntly.

"Why not?" I asked.

"Because when the fleet manager came in earlier to take away your old car he was disgusted with the state of it. He called me out to look at it and I was horrified. I don't think you should be allowed to mess another one up."

"It wasn't too bad, surely?" I said. "Just a few bits of rubbish I didn't have time to chuck out. I took all my CDs and other stuff out."

"Not too bad!" thundered Barry. "The passenger seat was covered in some sort of grease they couldn't get off. There were burger wrappers and other assorted shit everywhere. When I went to have a look, I was able to write my name in the dust on the dashboard, and to top it all, they found a fast-food chicken box under the seat full of rotting leftovers."

"So that's what the smell was," I said. "I did wonder. Still it's only a bit of mess, isn't it? That's what we have valeting for."

"It's a fucking disgrace, that's what it is," said Barry. "Are you going to trash this new car as well? You're a director now. What are clients going to think if you take them out? It's a car, not a skip."

"I have to travel around in my job a lot," I protested. "Sometimes I have to eat on the road. That's the nature of the work."

"Allow me to introduce you to something that you may find useful in the future," remarked Barry sarcastically, reaching under his desk and picking up the waste paper basket. "This is called a bin. You put rubbish into it. Clearly no one's ever taught you this, so now seems as good a time as any."

Eventually he let me have the keys to the new car, after he'd made me swear on my mother's life which was a bit harsh considering she was going to die in about a week's time. Perhaps he'd feel guilty about saying it when he found out.

With the BMW gone, I got acquainted with my "new" car, a Volvo, which, whilst not in the same league as what I had been used to, was still an extremely nice drive. I had to concede, looking around at the mess, he did have a point. As for the chicken bones, I eventually traced their origin back to Keele Services on the M6, when I got peckish on the way home from a meeting in Manchester four months earlier.

**July 2006**

A heatwave was spreading across the country, Lily Allen was top of the charts with a catchy little number entitled *Smile*, and I was out for a drink with Nick. The Turf Tavern was my favourite place to spend a summer evening in Oxford. As the night wore on, we worked our way down the list of guest ales on the blackboard behind the bar.

My father had died two weeks previously, and Nick had taken me out for the evening to try and cheer me up. It quickly transpired that he was the one that needed cheering up. He had just gone through a rather messy divorce and was feeling rather depressed about the fact that at 35 years old he already had two failed marriages behind him.

"At least we didn't have any kids," mused Nick.

"You were hardly with her long enough, really, were you?" I replied.

"No. I shouldn't have married her in the first place. I don't know what I was thinking of. Talk about love being blind. You must have suspected something."

Making a mental note that I would try and mention it when the time came, all I could offer, lamely, was "Sorry, mate". If I had said something, would it have made any difference, though? The world was full of people who thought their latest partner was the best thing since sliced bread, whilst all around them could see that they were in fact an arsehole. There was never any point saying anything, Nick was right: love was blind.

Fishing for details, I discovered that he'd picked her up in a nightclub in Oxford three years ago. Like myself, Nick had done very well within the company and after he took this girl home to his upmarket flat in Jericho, she took a real shine to him, or, as it later transpired, his money. Blinded to her selfish ways by her stunning figure, long legs, fake tan and plastic boobs, he had proposed within six months, desperate to keep hold of her.

They'd married in 2004 but had split up after about a year. She'd taken him for a mug and now possessed half of everything he'd had. That had included the flat, which had to be sold, and now he was renting a rather more modest pad somewhere off the Botley Road.

The conversation continued, with Nick's ranting increasing in line with the amount of beer he'd consumed.

"A hundred grand at least this has cost me. And she hardly ever wanted to have sex after we got married. Well, not with me, anyway."

That was a sore point. It seemed that they had split up after he'd found her in bed with a plumber who'd come to fix a burst pipe three months earlier. It turned out he'd been giving her pipes a good plumbing on a regular basis ever since. I had to feel a bit sorry for Nick. He seemed to be perennially unlucky in love.

He was still going on. "I was lucky if I got it once a month, mate. That's grand total of twelve shags from my second marriage. What's that, eight grand a shag or thereabouts? I'm a fucking idiot, I really am."

I thought it best not to mention to Nick that I'd once spent more than that on an all-nighter with two high-class escorts in a hotel in Mayfair. Instead I said, "She was hot, though. She must have been good in bed."

"Just because someone looks hot, doesn't mean they can cut it in the sack," he said. "She couldn't give head properly for a start. You use your lips and tongue, not your teeth. What's that all about? Didn't anyone ever tell her?"

"Perhaps they didn't like to complain, you know, looking a gift horse in the mouth and all that." I decided to change the subject before Nick started coming out with any more revelations about his unhappy sex life. "So, now that you've got the money from the flat, what are you going to do with it? Are you going to get another place?"

"No, I'm going to rent for a bit and see what happens to house prices. They've shot up the past few years. I reckon there's another crash on the way," said Nick, confidently.

"I wouldn't be so sure about that, Nick," I replied. Apart for a brief blip at the end of the decade, I knew that house prices would continue to rise at ridiculous rates for another fifteen years at least. "What are you going to do, then, put it into savings?"

"Well, I was going to," he said, "but then I went to see this bloke at the bank to talk about ISAs. He said that was a waste of time and that I'd be much better investing it all in the stock market. He showed me all sorts of graphs showing how much money the markets have made in the last few years, and I think it's worth a punt."

I had noticed when Nick had arrived that evening that he'd brought a copy of *The Times* along with him, and now I was about to find out why. Opening it out to the share pages, he excitedly showed me what he'd been doing.

"I've picked out a few stocks I like the look of," he said. "What do you think?"

I looked to see that he'd circled a number of companies with a yellow highlighter pen. I was horrified to discover that among the stocks he had picked out were Woolworths, Northern Rock and JJB Sports.

"Mate, this is a really, really bad idea," I said. "Trust me. You really don't know what might be around the corner," remembering the scenes in my head of Northern Rock's panicked customers queuing around the block to take their money out. "If you absolutely must put money into the stock market, put it into something bomb-proof like tobacco or pharmaceutical stocks."

"What could be safer than a bank?" asked Nick. "If your money's not safe with a bank, where is it safe: under the mattress?"

If only he knew, I thought, thinking of the financial crisis about to engulf the world. "You'd be surprised," I replied.

"And what about good old Woolies?" he added. "They've been around forever. They are as much a part of Britain as fish and chips."

Not for much longer, I thought. Seeing that he was determined to embark on this foolhardy venture, I thought I'd better at least try to minimise the damage. Sighing, I said, "OK, well at let's go through the share prices and see if we can come up with a decent portfolio."

By the time we'd finished I'd managed to steer him away from most of the companies that had gone bust, and point him in the direction of businesses that I knew would still be around in twenty years' time. Satisfied that I'd done my good deed for the day, and with him seemingly cheered up considerably, we got on with the serious business of drinking our way to the bottom of the blackboard.

A couple of weeks later I found myself waiting for my father to die in the very same hospital where I had breathed my last. There was a horrible air of déjà vu about the whole situation, and I didn't mean my usual day-to-day déjà vu. Like father, like son, he, too, was dying from lung cancer, having been a twenty a day man for over 40 years. He'd lasted longer than I had, though. Perhaps the love of my mother had kept him going, but even so, 66 was still too young to die.

He was in an awful state, a grey, pallid complexion, breathing through tubes and struggling to speak. This was exactly how I must have looked and I thought how awful it must have been for Stacey, especially with her mother already dead. Fortunately she was spared it all this time round. She was only seven years old now, and Sarah and I had both agreed she would be better off at school rather than seeing her beloved Grampy in this state. As he breathed his last, on a baking hot Monday afternoon, I had cause to reflect that for once, a death in the family had fallen outside the Christmas period.

In the weeks that preceded his death, his illness progressed incredibly quickly, just as mine had. He was also diagnosed only when it was way too late. To support my mother, I spent as much time with him as I could, which gave me yet more opportunities to find out about my earlier life. As summer turned to spring and he got better, we began to enjoy more and more family occasions. Sundays alternated between them coming to us for lunch and vice versa. Dad was also very much a pub man, and we started going out for a drink regularly, when he would sit in the pub and puff away to his heart's content. This was before the smoking ban, and sometimes we were joined by my uncle Bill, who liked nothing better than to sit on a bar stool, filling the air with the smoke from his pipe. Perhaps it was just as well that Dad had passed away when he had, as one of his major gripes was the government's plans to introduce a smoking ban in pubs. He considered this to be an infringement of his civil liberties.

When I'd died in 2025 there had only been Stacey left and I'd only seen her at weekends. It had been a lonely time but my journey back through time had now delivered me a wife, a mother and a father. With my family around me, I felt quite content, and if I could have stayed in that moment and gone back no further, I'd have been perfectly happy.

But time continued to march backwards, with me no more able to do anything about it than a normal person moving in the other direction. As it did so, I was watching Stacey growing younger before my eyes. She may have been the one who had been with me the longest, but I was more than aware that she would also be the first one whom I would lose.

**July 2005**

I had made a decision long ago not to get involved in events outside of my immediate friends and family. I knew that I could change things after the fire at the furniture store all those years in the future, but I was reluctant to intervene in other events. The news was regularly filled with stories of death and disaster, some of which could be prevented, some which couldn't.

If I'd tried to prevent every car crash, murder or terrorist outrage, I would never have found time to do anything else. Occasionally the idea of being a time-travelling detective, preventing crimes before they were committed, appealed, but was there really any point? And what right did I have to play God anyway? How would I choose who lived or died? If a teenager got killed because he got into a car driven by a joyriding mate, would it be alright to let him die because I was busy with some other more worthy cause at the other end of town? I didn't want to shoulder the responsibility of such decisions, so the vast majority of the time I allowed the world to play out as it was destined to.

However, in July 2005, I decided that I would make an exception to this rule. The first quarter of the 21st century had been peppered with one terrorist atrocity after another. In the days following each one, they dominated the news coverage.

It was when the terrorists came uncomfortably close to home, in the summer of 2005, that I began to wonder if there was anything I could do to prevent what occurred on that fateful morning of 7/7.

On that day, suicide bombers had exploded four bombs in the centre of London, three on Tube trains and one on a bus, killing 52 people. After careful consideration, I decided that I would try and warn the authorities in advance in the hope of preventing the attacks.

The Metropolitan Police had an anti-terrorist hotline, which I phoned at 7am on the morning of the attacks, nearly two hours before the first bomb went off.

I had planned very carefully what I was going to say. I needed to sound credible and convince them that this was a tangible threat. For all I knew, they might get dozens of calls a day from paranoid members of the public or hoaxers. I needed to ensure that they didn't think I was one of them.

I made the call from a phone box, one of many that seemed to have sprung up on the streets recently. I'd never seen anyone using them, everyone had mobile phones. Maybe that was why so many of them had disappeared in the future. They suited me very well for my purpose that day, though. I wanted anonymity to avoid any awkward questions later on.

So, when I rang, I also gave them a false name because I didn't want to be tracked down after the event. I calmly and concisely gave them the exact details of where and when each bomb would be set off, and the names of each of the bombers. When pressed on how I'd obtained this information, I told them I'd overheard two men discussing it in a pub in London the previous evening. When the questions began to become more probing, I put the phone down. Had I done the right thing? It wouldn't be long until I'd find out.

I went home, called the office to say I would not be coming in, and took Stacey to school. I hurried back home and switched on the 24-hour news channel.

As the news of the attacks broke, I was dismayed to discover that my call had achieved nothing. Everything had happened exactly as it had done before my intervention. Why hadn't they listened to me?

There was worse to come. Just before lunchtime, there was a hammering on the front door, accompanied by a shout of "Open up, this is the police." Before I could even get to the front door to open it, they smashed it down and came in, armed to the teeth, grabbing me and spreadeagling me against the wall.

I don't know how they had tracked me down. If their surveillance operations were as sophisticated as those I'd seen on TV, I guessed it hadn't been that difficult to find me. I was cuffed and taken off in the back of a van for questioning which wasn't what I'd had in mind at all. I'd tried to do a good thing, now I was being treated like a suspected terrorist myself.

These were not ordinary police, as I soon discovered as I wasn't being taken to the police station but to a high-security unit somewhere in London. Where, I had no idea as I had been handcuffed and led into the back of a van with blacked out windows. On arrival, I was then taken into an interrogation room and questioned. I was seriously shitting myself at this point. I had just recently finished watching the latest series of *24* on DVD (backwards like most series I watched) and I was uncomfortably aware of what they did to terrorist suspects to extract information, at least according to that show.

Thankfully, things did not go that far, but they did ask me some pretty hard-hitting questions. I stuck to my story that I'd overheard two men talking in a pub and eventually they seemed to accept it. I didn't fit the mould of the average terrorist who they probably had in their minds.

I had no doubt that my white skin and lack of any links to terrorist organisations had saved me from some more intensive methods. Would they have been as gentle on me if I'd been a Muslim of Middle Eastern origin? I didn't really want to think about it, the amount of prejudice in the world seemed to be getting worse as I travelled back through time, and I'd heard suggestions that in the past it had been rife within the authorities.

At 9pm, exhausted, I was released and I vowed never again to try and get involved in global events. I had saved no one and earned myself an extremely unpleasant day for my troubles. When 9/11 rolled around four years later, all I could do was watch helplessly as the Twin Towers fell, knowing there was nothing I could do to prevent it.

# Ibiza

### April 1999

I was at the hospital again, this time for what most would consider a happy event. For me, it was anything but. I was sitting by Sarah's bedside, awaiting the birth of my daughter. It seemed that it was to be the last time I would ever see her.

"They grow up so quickly" was a cliché I had heard many times over the years. If that was true, then so was the reverse. It seemed like no time at all since Stacey had left home to live with David and now here she was, back in her mother's womb, preparing to emerge.

I had enjoyed growing younger with her at first: helping her with her homework, building sandcastles on the beach, and all the other things that had filled my life with joy on a daily basis. The best times had been when she was around four or five years old. She was so cute and clever, amusing me no end with her observations on the world in the way that only a wide-eyed, open-minded child could. But as she'd grown younger still, I'd begun to find the whole process quite heartbreaking.

I'd watched as she'd lost the ability to write, and then to read. Her speech became progressively less coherent, and as she approached two years of age, I found myself changing my first nappy. It was not dissimilar to the process Sarah had been through with her mother a few years previously. She had suffered from Alzheimer's and had required more and more care as time had moved forward. That at least was a natural process, and, awful as it had been for Sarah, at least it had happened in the right order.

Watching it happen to Stacey from my perspective was something no one else could possibly understand.

As she regressed towards her first birthday, she lost the ability to walk and talk. She could still smile and giggle as I played with her during the first year of her life, but even that stopped eventually in the last few weeks before her birth. It was very hard seeing her as a newborn, oblivious to pretty much everything, reduced to crying for her basic needs, nappy changes and suckling on Sarah's nipples.

She was around six months of age when Sarah and I married. We didn't have a lavish wedding, just a registry office and a quiet reception at a village hall a few miles outside of Oxford. The fact that we'd had a baby together hadn't been the main reason behind our decision to wed. I am pretty sure we would have married regardless; we must have both known we had found the right one. Apparently I'd proposed the day after Stacey had been born, so I made sure that I played things out exactly as they were meant to. At least I didn't have to worry about where to get the ring from on the day of the proposal: it was already conveniently waiting for me in my coat pocket.

I knew that once Stacey was gone, she would exist only in my mind. There would be no photographs, and no one to reminisce with about her. She would simply cease to exist. My beautiful daughter, who had nursed me through my cancer and been ever-present by my side for so many years, would be gone forever. It was a very depressing thought, and I had to make the utmost effort to seem excited for Sarah's sake as she went into labour.

I had grown used to things disappearing forever, but they had been mostly material objects up until now. They were things that I'd learnt to live without. My mobile phone got downgraded every year, getting bigger and clunkier each time. 4G and 3G were long since gone; the last phone I'd had that could access the internet had something called WAP on it, which was laughably poor. The latest one even had an aerial that I had to pull out to make a call. From home I found that I could only get a signal on it by leaning out of the bedroom window.

Music was a big part of my life which was gradually being taken away from me piece by piece. I used to plug my iPod into my car via the USB port on long business trips, or listen to it through the headphones when I was flying abroad. I loved the indie rock bands of the mid-2000s like The Kaiser Chiefs, The Kooks and Keane, but by 2003 they were all gone from the device. I could still hear the songs in my head, but that was the only place they existed now. The bands had not even written them yet.

On the plus side, the day was rapidly approaching when I'd never have to hear Westlife on the radio ever again, so there were some consolations. As for the iPod itself, I saw it for the last time on Christmas Day 2002, my present from Sarah. After that I had to make do with CDs.

These were minor annoyances, though, all of which I could live with, insignificant in comparison with the loss of my daughter who was irreplaceable. Coming into the world at 1am, I had just three hours to say goodbye, before I was whisked away by my 4am curfew, my days as a parent now over. If having to deal with the fact that I would never see Stacey again wasn't bad enough, I also had to face up to the fact that, in less than a year, Sarah would be gone, too.

**July 1998**

Sarah and I had met on holiday in Ibiza in July 1998, proving the exception to the rule that holiday romances never last. Nick, reeling from the break-up of his first marriage, had persuaded me that we needed to go on a Club 18-30 holiday while we were still young enough. I doubt whether I would have needed much persuasion at that point in my life. I knew that I had been single for over a year before I'd met Sarah.

As I travelled back through the nine months prior to Stacey's birth, I managed to piece together the details of how we'd gone from holiday romance to doting parents in so short a time.

When Stacey had been about a year old, we had moved house from the modest starter home I'd bought on the Greater Leys development to the east of the city. The starter home was a tiny, one-bedroomed place, referred to by Sarah as "the Shoebox". It was fine when Stacey was a baby, but as she grew we needed to find somewhere bigger. I was a rising star at Head Office by this time, acquiring the role of Senior Market Research Executive before I turned 30, enabling me to easily afford the new house in North Oxford which had been my home for over a quarter of a century afterwards. As winter 1998 turned to autumn, at four months pregnant, Sarah had moved into the shoebox with me in time for Christmas.

Her Welsh accent was much stronger in those days than in later years. All those years of living in England had softened it considerably. One of the first things I'd fallen in love with was her voice, and that had never diminished: her lilting Welsh tones never failed to thrill me.

After we'd met in Ibiza, we'd sworn to keep in touch. Our holidays had overlapped by a week on either side, so she didn't fly back until a week after I got home. During that week, she had sent me postcards every day, none of which had arrived back in the UK before she did. We were in the early stages of the mobile era now, and quite a lot of people didn't have them yet, Sarah included. As for landlines, calls to and from abroad were far more expensive and unreliable than they had been in the 21$^{st}$ century. We hadn't been able to bear being apart and out of touch, so true to the story she'd related to me, I made sure I was at Cardiff Airport, complete with a bunch of flowers, to meet her off the plane on her return.

We had spent every weekend together throughout the late summer, having more sex than I'd ever had in my life. We barely got out of bed some weekends, getting takeaway pizzas and watching the *Brookside* omnibus on Channel 4 after the racing on Saturday afternoons. I'd participated very enthusiastically, knowing that it was going to result in her getting pregnant. It was on the last weekend of September when she'd excitedly shown me the pregnancy kit with two blue lines showing in the box. Potentially any weekend before that could have been the moment that we hit the jackpot. I got very excited every time at the thought of a microscopic mini-Stacey (or half of her anyway) swimming up Sarah's cervix, ready to hit the target.

When we worked out the dates, we came to the conclusion that she must have got pregnant either on, or very shortly after, the holiday. Presumably I hadn't used condoms when we'd slept together in Ibiza, despite all the general advice to do so. I had never been very keen on the things, and although I knew I'd had them with me on the holiday (I found an unused pack in my suitcase when I unpacked), clearly I hadn't been asked to use them, so hadn't bothered. Irresponsible it may have been, but since it had led to the creation of my beloved Stacey, I wasn't going to worry about it.

The final week before I got to Ibiza dragged by, especially with Sarah already over there and out of contact. Finally the day arrived, and I awoke to find myself with her, on two twin beds we had pushed together in an extremely basic hotel room.

Nick and I had been sharing a room, but he'd generously agreed to take one for the team and paired up with Sarah's rather less attractive friend, Sam. He didn't seem too fussy. He hadn't had a lot of action since his divorce, or on the first week of the holiday, so he wasn't going to look a gift horse in the mouth. I knew he was going to drop her like a ton of bricks when we got back to the UK.

I savoured every single moment of that final glorious week together, knowing it was to be our last. When we had sex, I was more enthusiastic than I'd ever been, willing my little swimmers on towards their target. I even turned down her offers of blow jobs, wanting to make sure I kept her topped up as much as possible. As I'd suspected, the subject of condoms was never mentioned.

We dined out, went clubbing, and in the daytimes either chilled at the beach or took part in some of the outrageous activities the club reps had organised. Beach parties with highly dubious games that involved licking cream off people, huge amounts of alcohol, and organised trips out to various nightspots in and around San Antonio made the week go by extremely quickly. It was full-on in every sense, or "having it large", as the reps liked to call it.

Inevitably the final day arrived, the one when I would meet Sarah for the first time. It was the middle Saturday of a two-week holiday for me, but she was only due to fly in that afternoon. Expecting to wake up alone, I was extremely surprised to be woken up that morning by a red-headed Scottish girl, of whose existence I had been previously unaware. She was extremely pretty and very lively, having woken me up by reaching down beneath the sheets and grabbing hold of me, her intentions abundantly clear.

This didn't feel right at all. Here I was, preparing to meet the love of my life for the last time, and I was being very vigorously and very enthusiastically stirred into action by someone else. It felt rather like cheating, a term I wasn't particularly keen on, but it fitted the scenario. Technically it wasn't cheating, after all, I hadn't actually met Sarah yet, but even so, I felt pretty uncomfortable with the whole situation.

My body had no such qualms, though, responding proudly to her attentions, and when she leapt on top of me, I just let nature take its course.

Her name was Cathy, and I didn't have much time to get to know her. It had been a one-night thing, and she was due to get on a plane back to Glasgow that very afternoon.

We may have exchanged bodily fluids, but we didn't exchange numbers. She wasn't that sort of girl. By 11am she was safely on her way to the airport, and I was safe in the knowledge that I'd never see or hear from her again because I hadn't, other than on the previous evening, obviously, when we'd somehow ended up in bed together.

Every Saturday night, the reps arranged a welcome tour of San Antonio's bars for the latest batch of holidaymakers. Although Nick and I had already been there a week, he suggested we went along to check out the new recruits. He was not in the best of moods at the midway point of the holiday. Not only had he failed miserably to pull after a week, he'd also had to sleep on one of the sunbeds by the pool the previous night, after I'd taken Cathy back to the room.

"Some holiday this is turning out to be," he grumbled, as we got ready to go out for the evening. "I've been here a week and I haven't even had a sniff of a shag yet. Remember what Pizza Dave said to us in The Duke last week? If you can't get a shag in Ibiza, you won't get one anywhere. Well, it doesn't bode well for my future sex life, does it?"

"Don't panic," I said, adding confidently, "I'm pretty sure your luck is about to change. There's a whole new batch of girls down there that have flown in today looking for sun, sea and sex. We've been here a week now, we're old hands. Tonight's the night, I reckon."

"That's easy for you to say," he replied, making no attempt to hide his jealousy. "You got it last night. I had to sleep by the pool because of you, and all I've got to show for it is a load of mosquito bites." As he spoke, he was spraying himself very generously with Joop! to cover up the smell of the antihistamine cream he'd smeared all over his bites.

"I'd go easy on that if I were you," I said. "You're meant to use it sparingly, not go around smelling like you've had a bath in it."

"Better safe than sorry," he said, adding some deodorant to the mix. "It gets pretty hot and sweaty in those bars."

He had a point. It was mid-July in Ibiza, and absolutely sweltering. I decided to spray a bit of extra deodorant on myself. I didn't want Sarah's first impression of me to be of some bloke with B.O.

Soon we were ready: two smartly dressed young men ready to paint San Antonio red. We were to meet in the bar downstairs at 8.30pm. Although the event had been put on for the new arrivals, no one had said we couldn't go. Nick had done it all before, but I hadn't, so technically, in my eyes, I was a new arrival, too.

I knew for a fact that Sarah and Sam would be down there in the bar, but I also knew that we wouldn't actually start talking until we got to the first bar in town. She had recounted the tale of how we'd first met many times, which was just as well, since I couldn't remember it. All I needed to do now was stick to the script.

We headed downstairs. I was eager to get my first glimpse of my future bride, and sure enough, there she was, long, golden hair cascading down over a light blue dress that came down to just above her knees, chatting to Sam.

I steered us over towards them, curious to see if I could catch her eye. She glanced in our direction, but looked straight through us as if we weren't even there. It seemed I hadn't left much of an initial impression, even though Sarah had sworn blind to me in years ahead that it had been love at first sight.

So, I bided my time until we got to the first bar, where our oft-recalled first meeting had happened. We left the hotel in a large group and the reps led us out of the hotel, through the streets, and towards the music square in the centre of town. It was a vibrant, buzzing place with touts on every corner desperately trying to tempt the punters into one of the dozens of bars that lined the narrow streets with their various offers. It seemed that the BOGOF concept wasn't something that was just confined to supermarkets.

I made sure we held back a little and walked just behind Sarah and Sam so I could listen to their conversation. They were babbling away excitedly in their Welsh accents, talking about Es Paradis, one of the main clubs in San Antonio. The four of us had been there already, on Wednesday afternoon when they'd held a water party on the dance floor, so I made a mental note to enthuse about it when we got talking. I couldn't hear a great deal of what they were saying as I had Nick babbling on in my ear about some other bar he'd heard about where you could drink as much as you wanted in an hour for 1,000 pesetas.

"We'll go there tomorrow," I answered, annoyed at his attempts to derail my plans for the evening. "I want to stick with the rest of the group tonight, give us a chance to meet some of the new people."

When we got to the bar, there were not many people there, but it soon filled up. All of the Club 18-30 holidaymakers from all of the hotels had convened in the same place, and before long it was "banging", another favourite word of the reps. There was a dance floor area at the back and as we ordered our drinks the music began playing, a recent hit from Run-DMC vs Jason Nevins blasting out from the sound system.

Sarah and Sam had moved over to the edge of the dance floor. They'd ordered a fishbowl, full of Tequila Sunrise, and had placed it on a chest-high table at the edge of the floor. They were tapping their feet to the music as they swiftly drained the bowl through their straws. Nick and I both had pints of lager. I wasn't a huge lager fan, but clubs and bars in Ibiza didn't tend to cater for real ale enthusiasts. I gestured towards them, and said to Nick, "Hey, what do you reckon to those two?"

He looked across and said, "Yeah, she's well, tasty. The blonde one, that is. Don't fancy yours much, though."

I thought he was being a bit harsh. OK, Sam was a little chubby, with freckles and frizzy dark hair, but she wasn't that bad. She'd ultimately ended up being Sarah's bridesmaid at our wedding, which had been a little uncomfortable for Nick who was best man. I didn't see Sam much after that because she drifted out of our lives once Sarah settled permanently in Oxford. She was a nice enough girl, but Nick wasn't very keen on her.

After the holiday, she'd tried to keep in touch with him, but he didn't want to know. He'd never mentioned the fact that he'd fancied Sarah before, though. Perhaps he'd stepped aside once I'd beaten him to it. Looking at the way he was eyeing her up now, I realised I was going to have to make my move before he tried anything. I couldn't have the whole of the next 27 years being changed by something as trivial as letting him speak to her first.

"Don't you mean yours, mate?" I replied, "I saw them first, I'm calling shotgun," and I strode quickly across towards them.

"Hang on a minute," he tried to protest but it was too late, I was committed. Destiny was calling and there was nothing he could do about it.

After that, it all went swimmingly. I offered to buy her a drink, got chatting, drank heavily as we moved from bar to bar, and eventually ended up in a drunken snog in Es Paradis. It was already gone 3am by this time, which didn't leave me much longer with her. My curfew on European time at this time of year was 5am, and I was relieved when she jumped at the suggestion we go back to the hotel early.

When I broke the news to Nick, that I wanted to take her back to the room, he wasn't particularly happy. "What are you like?" he asked. "You put one on a plane back to Glasgow this morning, and now you've picked up one from Wales! What is this, a tour of the British Isles?"

So, for the second night in a row, Nick found himself shut out of the room, but at least he had a willing partner to have some fun with this time. After a little persuasion from me, I suggested that he go back with Sam, who was clearly keen on him. He moaned about it to begin with, but when I reminded him about his earlier complaints about the lack of sex, including my use of the expression "beggars can't be choosers", he relented and went back to the girls' room with Sam.

This left me with barely an hour. I savoured every last curve of Sarah's body for the final time, as she enjoyed mine for the first.

The bedside clock read 4.59am, as I cuddled up in her arms, ready to be whisked away at any moment. I moved in closer and whispered "goodbye" into her ear. Seconds later, the room vanished, and I found myself on the middle of the dance floor in a club I didn't recognise, another huge summer tune from The Tamperer blasting out all around me.

She was gone. And there was nothing I could do about it. I took solace in some drunken, joyless sex with Cathy that night, but nothing could ease the pain of losing Sarah.

### September 1995

My twenties progressed backwards, seemingly one long party. I worked hard and played hard. My body was young and fit and it seemed I could effortlessly go out and drink several pints at night and still be as fresh as a daisy for work in the morning. By this time I was no longer at head office but working as an assistant manager in one of the superstores. I was on about £15,000 a year which didn't sound a lot compared to what I had been used to, but it was more than enough for me to get a mortgage on a house in 1995. So, at the tender age of 24, I became a homeowner. Of course, for me, this meant the end of independence and moving back in with my parents in Botley.

I'd paid just £39,000 for the house, which turned out to be one of the best investments I had ever made. There had been a prolonged slump in the housing market since a price crash at the start of the decade. With a recession following, houses were remarkably cheap. It was a completely different scenario from the early decades of the next century. By 2020, it would not be possible to buy even a one-bedroomed house in Oxford for less than £200,000, putting homeownership completely out of the reach of most local young people. I'd had no way of knowing this when I'd bought the house the first time round: it seemed that I'd made a remarkably shrewd decision, but the reality was, I'd just got lucky with the timing.

I had lived in my starter home for five years, so it seemed odd when the day of my arrival approached. On the day after I'd moved in, I found the place full of boxes containing the sum total of my life's possessions. There were records, cassette tapes and CDs galore. There were at least four big boxes full of video cassettes which took up a ridiculous amount of room compared to the DVDs I'd later owned. One series of *Star Trek* comprised thirteen videotapes alone and took up the whole top shelf of the video cabinet I'd kept them in. According to the price stickers on them, I'd paid £9.99 per tape from somewhere called Our Price. This seemed outrageous compared to the DVD box sets containing an entire season which had barely cost me a tenner on the internet a decade or so later and took up a fraction of the space.

I had got used to prices getting cheaper over the years. Petrol and food were half the price now that they had been in 2010. Clearly when it came to home entertainment, the reverse was true. Perhaps that was one of the reasons why the pubs were so busy now; there was less to do at home and it was more expensive. I also noticed that the price of drink seemed to have declined rapidly in pubs to a point where it was now quite competitive compared to supermarket prices. Nick and I were paying less than 2 quid a pint to drink in Oxford now, and it seemed to be dropping by at least 10p a year. The price of beer in the supermarkets meanwhile didn't seem to be getting any cheaper.

Whilst I was sorting through some of the boxes, I came across an old Victorian biscuit tin which I hadn't seen before. I certainly didn't remember seeing it when Sarah and I had moved into the big house in North Oxford, so where it had gone by then I had no idea. Curious, I opened it, and inside I found a veritable treasure trove of letters and keepsakes.

There was a whole bunch of letters bound tightly by an elastic band. It was obvious from the back of the envelopes, smothered in hearts and kisses, and the faint scent of perfume, that they were love letters. Fascinated, I opened them to discover that they were written in French. Fortunately my French was good, I'd taken it at A Level, according to my CV, and I had no difficulty at all in reading them.

"*Mon cher Thomas*," began the first one, and I eagerly read on.

The letters spanned a period of about a year, from August 1987 to July 1988. They were passionate, romantic and beautifully written in old-fashioned ink upon scented coloured paper. I had lived my life through an era of social media, texting and email so it was a joy to handle these real, handwritten letters. There were pictures, too, of a very pretty and dark-haired girl who could not have been more than sixteen.

The girl's name was Simone, and it seemed that, just as with Sarah, I had met her on holiday, this time in France in the summer of 1987. She lived in a small village near Rennes, and the passionate nature of her writing left me in no doubt as to the intensity of our relationship.

Clearly the letters had been the only way we had been able to keep in touch. The internet was primitive enough now in 1995, and mobile phones were the preserve only of the very wealthy or ostentatious. By 1987, both would have disappeared. Disappointingly, it seemed I'd never seen Simone again after that first summer, the letters fizzling out over time.

Clearly I must have felt something for her, if only I could see the letters I had written to her I might have been able to see just how much. Bearing in mind that I, too, would be sixteen in 1987, there was a very real chance that this was not only my first love, but also the girl to whom I had lost my virginity.

My life always seemed to have more purpose when I had something to look forward to, and my fascination with Simone would grow and grow over the eight years that would pass before I would finally meet her.

# Josh

**February 1991**

It was proving to be a bitterly cold month across Oxfordshire. I was noticing it more than most, because now I was working as an assistant manager for a newsagent's in Botley. This meant starting work at 5.30am in the morning when it was bloody cold.

More often than not my car, a horrible, mustard-coloured 1978 Austin Maxi, wouldn't start, leaving me having to trudge to work through the freezing ice and snow to open the shop. It was a pain having to open the shop that early in the morning as there was hardly ever anyone about. The main reason it had to be done was for the papers. I had noticed as the years had passed that people were less and less inclined to get milk and papers from supermarkets and preferred to have them delivered. Suddenly there was an army of milk floats on the road, not to mention eager teenagers willing to risk life and limb lugging *The Sunday Times* around.

I had to mark all of the papers up by hand for the rounds, ready for the paper boys to take out. They started to arrive around 6.30am, so I needed to have it finished by then.

The paper boys did not get paid very much for the thankless task of delivering these papers in all weathers. For taking out the morning papers seven days a week and the *Oxford Mail* on six afternoons, they received the princely sum of £15. I soon noticed that several of them liked to top up their earnings by filling their bags with bars of chocolate and sweets when they thought I wasn't looking. I was pretty eagle-eyed, though, and confiscated anything I caught them trying to shoplift, usually eating it myself after they'd gone.

Once I'd caught one of them, I could catch him every day after that, as I'd know his methods. The company policy was instant dismissal for anyone caught shoplifting, but I wasn't that daft. I knew if I sacked one of them that there would be no one to do their round that day which would lead to a string of angry calls from customers demanding to know where their papers were. On top of that, I'd have to take the round out myself once one of the shop assistants arrived at 9am, as opposed to sitting in my cosy office drinking coffee and reading *Viz*. My standard procedure was therefore to let them off with a warning and pocket the contraband.

It wasn't just the paper boys doing the pilfering. Several of the staff had their own little scams going as well. We used to get a regular tobacco delivery on Monday afternoons, and I'd noticed that my fellow assistant manager, Colin, was always most keen to take that shift. He was most perturbed when the delivery driver was changed, so I decided to do a little detective work to find out what had been going on when the previous Monday rolled around. It seemed that a 200 pack of B&H was conveniently "falling off the back of the lorry" each week into Colin's lap, with a £10 note going the other way. Perhaps that was why they had changed the delivery driver: he must have been caught.

Meanwhile, my assistant, Jenny, a middle-aged, married woman who manned the tills in the mornings, liked nothing better than to "accidentally" open a bag of crisps while stocking up the shelves and then announce that, as it was now damaged stock and we couldn't sell it, she might as well eat it.

Overall, I enjoyed working at the shop. The office out the back was my own little kingdom where I could do whatever I wanted and it was good fun out on the shop floor most of the time. Apart from the occasional miserable git moaning because Mars bars had gone up to 24p and that sort of thing, I enjoyed lots of banter with the regular customers and the staff. Some of the pensioners treated the shop a bit like a social club and would hang around rambling on for hours about nothing in particular. The favourite topics of conversation seemed to be hip replacements, the war, the youth of today, and the fact that the new 5p piece was too fiddly. I found it all quite entertaining and played along accordingly.

Another thing I found amusing was serving the teenage boys who came in looking extremely nervous, hanging around by the magazines, casting furtive glances at the top shelf. I used to have a bit of fun at their expense, coming out with comments like "Jazz mag, is it? What do you fancy, *Escort* or *Razzle*?", leading to lots of stammered responses and red faces. Still, perhaps I shouldn't have taken the piss so much. I might well be doing the same in a few years' time when my supply of the real thing would have well and truly dried up.

Financially, things were looking a bit woeful for me around this time. The job at the newsagent paid a pittance compared to what I had been used to and I frequently found myself skint, despite living at home with my parents. It seemed that I spent most of my nights frittering away my cash in the pub. There wasn't much in the way of home entertainment to keep me in. My parents liked to watch TV most evenings in the living room, detective dramas and sitcoms for the most, but I found that pretty boring. I'd seen most of these shows decades later on Freeview. I had a TV in my room, but it was only a 16" portable and we didn't have Sky which was in its infancy at the time. Faced with the four measly channels available or a night at the pub, I usually chose the latter. I did have a Sega Megadrive, but that was primitive compared to the consoles I'd been used to, and as for the internet, no one had even heard of it. About the most advanced technological feature I had available to me now was CEEFAX on my telly, and that was laughably slow. Sitting watching the little numbers tick around to flick on to the next page was painful.

So, the pub it was. I was a local at a good, old-fashioned boozer close to home and spent most nights in there with a gang of like-minded young men. The main activities seemed to be pool, darts and playing on the one-armed bandits. I really couldn't see the point of those machines. They swallowed money like no tomorrow that could be better spent on beer, and the jackpot was pitiful. It was just £4.80 and that came out in tokens that you had to put back in anyway. Despite that, my friends seemed to love playing them and presumably I had, too, judging by the state of my bank account. My future knowledge was of absolutely no practical use whatsoever when it came to predicting the outcome of a three-reel slot machine, so I avoided playing them, regardless of what I'd done in my past life.

With my bank account constantly overdrawn, I was struggling to obtain cash. There were numerous occasions when I faced the dreaded "Insufficient Funds Available" message when attempting to withdraw money from the cashpoint.

Under the circumstances, I had no choice but to begin patronising the bookies again. Conveniently, there was one located a couple of doors along from the newsagent's, so I'd often leave Jenny in charge of the shop for ten minutes and nip out to put a bet on. Learning from past mistakes, I tried not to get too greedy. A simple 10p Yankee on four moderately priced winners each day was enough for my needs. Picking up £50 or so after work provided more than enough cash for the evening's entertainment, perhaps a bit more if I was taking a girl out. If I was totally skint I used to borrow the stake money out of the till. I could always put it back later.

So that was my worklife in my early twenties. As for my love life, it seemed that, prior to meeting Sarah, I hadn't really settled with any of the girlfriends that I'd had. Life was a succession of short relationships, never more than a year, interspersed with shorter periods of being single. Each new girlfriend who came along provided a welcome distraction from the tedium of everyday life, as well as taking care of my sexual needs, but I didn't feel particularly enamoured of any of them. They just weren't Sarah, that was all there was to it. I missed her terribly, thinking about her all the time and wondering what she was doing. So often I felt tempted to drive down to Wales and find her, but decided against it. What would be the point? I could only see her briefly, she'd have no idea who I was and it would only cause fresh heartbreak for me. I just had to try and get on with life and forget both her and Stacey.

My one consoling thought was that the day of my appointment with Josh was fast approaching. If, and it was a big if, he had unlocked the secret of time travel, would he remember me? Would he be there on August the 6th 1990? The date had been etched in my brain for over 30 years. Unfortunately, I was about to discover that my plans to meet him on that day were in serious danger of being thwarted.

**August 1990**

It was in early September that I realised I had made a schoolboy error in picking an August date for meeting up with Josh.

My parents had been reminiscing for some time about the fantastic holiday we'd had. When the holiday snaps came back from the chemist's and my tan started to develop, the sudden realisation dawned that I could have a clash of dates to deal with. I rushed to the calendar on the wall in the kitchen where my mother recorded anything and everything, flicked it back over to the August page and was confronted with the news I had feared. From the 30th of July to the 13th of August, we'd been on holiday on the Greek island of Paxos.

What was I to do? There was no way of getting out of this one. I was going to wake up on the 6th of August on the other side of Europe, needing to be back in Oxford by 5pm. How was I going to do it? Would I have the money and means to make such a journey? Was it even worth bothering? It was somewhat of a long shot that Josh would even be there in the first place. He hadn't been at all confident that he would be able to discover the secret of time travel and to my knowledge, no one else ever had. The only concrete evidence I had that there was any possibility of it at all was my own backwards existence, and even that wasn't anything I had any control over.

In the end I decided that I had to try. It was the only possible way I would ever get answers to the questions that I sought. Without those answers, my mind would never be at ease. Had the things I had done made a difference? Did I live on beyond 2025, and if so, was I happy? I had one chance, a slim possibility, maybe, but it was the only chance I had so my mind was made up. I would make it back to Oxford by 5pm that day no matter what it took. I was a man on a mission.

Being in Paxos immediately put me at a disadvantage over most Greek islands. It had no airport, so it was a two-hour ferry journey to Corfu before I'd even be able to think about getting a flight. I also had the familiar problem of not knowing what time I was going to wake up in the morning. What if I'd been drinking heavily the night before and didn't wake up until lunchtime? This had been the case on more than one occasion already during the week I had spent there.

I checked the ferry timetables. There was one at 7.30am, and the next one at 9.45am. I really needed to be on that first one, but I knew the odds were against me, and so it was proved when I awoke, just after 9am. Fortunately my parents were still asleep, which spared me any lengthy explanations.

I didn't want to worry them, so I hastily scribbled down a note and left it on the tiny kitchen table:

*Met a girl in a taverna last night, and gone on a trip to Corfu. Back tomorrow, love Tom.*

They would be annoyed, but hopefully that would be all. I left all of my clothes and my suitcase: I wouldn't need them. The only thing I needed was my passport and hopefully they wouldn't think to look for it.

My father's wallet was on the table next to where I left the note. It was bloated with drachmas. One of the things I liked about the Greek currency was that the notes went down to really small denominations, as low as 50 drachmas which equated to about 20p. It was easy to feel rich in Paxos, flashing the huge wads around even on my relatively meagre holiday funds.

I was tempted to take some because what I had was nowhere near enough to get me home, but consequences or not, I could not bring myself to steal from my own parents. I'd have to look for some other opportunity en route.

I walked quickly down the stony path between the olive trees that led towards the harbour, the sun already hot on my skin even at this early hour. There were plenty of people getting onto the ferry, including several English tourists laden with suitcases, none of whom I recognised. That was a good sign. That meant they must be going home today, and that meant that there would be at least one flight back to the UK that I could try and get myself on. Quite how, I wasn't sure. What if they were all fully booked?

Once I was on the boat, I spent some time wandering around the deck, sussing out the other passengers. Paxos wasn't an obvious package holiday destination so there were not many family groups. It was mainly couples and quite a few singles. I got chatting to a few, and it turned out they were all on the same flight, the 1.15pm to Manchester. That wasn't much use to me. I was pretty sure that it would be full, being a package holiday flight and even if I could get on it, Manchester was a long way from Oxford. I also still had very little money.

Fortunately, that was about to change. I really didn't like stealing, despite the endless opportunities available to me. Nicking the odd bar of chocolate from the newsagent's was one thing. Stealing some poor guy's wallet was quite another. Fortunately, my reservations about doing so were quite laid to rest when I encountered the most unpleasant pair of holidaymakers I had ever come across.

Jim and Sandra were from Salford, and as I walked around the deck of the boat, I could hear him moaning from a mile off in his broad Mancunian accent.

"Worst bloody holiday ever," he was going on. "Disgusting food, no proper beach and you can't even flush the toilet paper down the bog."

His wife was just as bad, bemoaning the lack of a McDonald's. I listened as they recanted one complaint after another. What the hell had they come here for, I wondered. Presumably they must normally go to Benidorm or somewhere like that. Whatever possessed them to choose Paxos?

My experience had been completely at odds with theirs. All of the food I'd had on the island had been amazing. Most of it was home-cooked by family-run restaurants, some of which seemed to amount to little more than a couple of tables in someone's back garden. It was all traditional Greek food, such as taramasalata and plenty of freshly caught fish. The swordfish steaks I'd eaten had been awesome. A fishing boat came into the harbour each morning and the fisherman would throw a couple of swordfish out onto the harbour front. He'd jump off the boat, chop it into steaks with a hefty cleaver in front of a circle of onlookers, and then the various restaurant owners would buy what they wanted from him there and then, ready to cook that night. You don't get much fresher than that. But presumably Jim and Sandra would rather have had cod and chips.

The two had to be seen to be believed. I'd seen stereotypical characters moaning about foreigners in reruns of old 70s sitcoms. I hadn't believed such people really existed until now.

"I'm going up to get a beer," said Jim. "Probably that Amstel rubbish as usual. I can't wait to get back to the Queens for a proper pint."

I watched him go up to the bar, wallet sticking out of the back pocket of his ridiculously tight Bermuda shorts that were at least two sizes too small for his fat arse. It looked like it was bulging with cash which surprised me, considering that it was the last day of his holiday. This was too good an opportunity to miss. He had money, and he was also an arsehole. I could steal from him, conscience clear. I sauntered up casually behind him, watched him take out his wallet to order his beer, and then slip it back in the same place. With a slight deft of hand, I swiped his wallet without him or anyone else noticing and quickly walked to the other end of the boat.

I didn't have long; surely he would notice the wallet was missing when he sat down. They were sitting near the bow of the boat, and I was now safely at the stern. Quickly I opened the wallet and was delighted to discover that the majority of the notes in it were not Greek at all, but good old sterling. The bloke had more money than sense. Why was he walking around with so much British currency on him? Presumably he was just one of those types who always felt the need to have a load of cash on them to wave around to show everyone how wealthy they were. Whatever the reason, it was his loss and my gain.

I took out all the cash, at least £500, and a decent amount of drachmas as well. Making sure no one was looking, I tossed the wallet over the back of the boat straight into the Aegean Sea, just as a right hullabaloo erupted behind me.

"Hey, someone's stolen my wallet!" I heard Jim exclaim, and watched from a safe distance as he kicked off in no uncertain terms. He didn't do himself any favours at all, especially when he started accusing the "thieving Greek bastard" behind the bar. He got no support whatsoever from the other holidaymakers who clearly found him as irritating as I did; thus his demands to have everyone searched fell on deaf ears. Not that it would have done any good anyway; there was nothing on the cash in my pocket to link it back to him.

Watching him rant and rave, getting redder in the face by the minute, was quite amusing. He really was a horrible, fat little man and I felt almost as if I'd done the world a favour by dealing him a misfortune. He well and truly deserved it.

Docking at Corfu, I had no time to lose. I certainly wasn't going to waste time waiting for a bus to the airport, and grabbed the first taxi I saw. At 11.45am, I practically ran into the departure lounge, scanning the boards for a flight back to England. Other than the Manchester flight, now delayed until 2.20pm, there was nothing until the evening: far too late for me. A quick enquiry at the check-in desk confirmed what I'd already suspected – the Manchester flight was full anyway.

I wasn't beaten yet. I had a plan B. Corfu was predominantly a holiday airport when it came to international flights, invariably fully booked. However, I could get an internal flight to Athens and there was one scheduled for 12.40pm. I quickly changed some of Jim's sterling into drachmas at the bureau de change and headed for the booking desk. I was in luck. The Athens flight was used mainly by Greeks who worked in the islands, going to and fro on business, and there were plenty of spare seats. I knew once I got to Athens Airport I'd have a much better chance of getting a flight home, as they would have many more flights that were not purely dedicated to holidaymakers.

The plane was in the air on time, and the flight to Athens took just one hour. I had no luggage and there were no customs, so getting through the airport was easy. Well before 2pm, I was in Athens Airport, scanning the boards for the flight that I hoped would take me home. My luck held. I had been hoping for a flight to Gatwick, but I was delighted to see that there was a British Airways flight to Heathrow, much closer to Oxford. It didn't take off until 3pm, though, and I had to meet Josh at 5pm.

Luckily, Greece was two hours ahead of the UK, so I could still make it. The flight time was only two hours, and I had just enough drachmas left to cover it. I hadn't changed all the sterling I'd lifted from Jim because I knew that I'd still need some at the other end.

With the flight taking off only ten minutes behind schedule, I was able to relax for the first time that day. It was less than six hours since I'd got on the boat from Paxos and now I was on a flight bound for home. I was really beginning to believe that I was going to make it. But would Josh be there? I'd hate it if I'd gone to all this effort for nothing.

It seemed to take an age to land at Heathrow where we were stuck in a stacking system above the airport. I put my watch back two hours before we landed and checked it as I cleared customs with no problems. It was 3.27pm. I rushed out of the airport and enquired at the taxi rank how much it would be for a black cab. Needless to say, it was beyond my means, I had only around £40 left after paying for the flights. I toyed with the idea of stealing a car, but it was too risky and would be stacking up potential problems later on. In the end, I jumped on a National Express coach bound for Oxford and hoped for the best.

The journey went well, to begin with. We were ahead of the rush hour, and the M40 was running smoothly. As we headed past the Park and Ride on the outskirts of Oxford, it was 4.39pm. With only around three miles to go, I really did think I was going to make it.

And then we hit the Oxford traffic. It was queued up to the Headington roundabout, and then at a crawl through Headington itself. By the time we got to St Clement's, there was less than five minutes left. I was getting frantic, checking my watch every few seconds. As we crawled over Magdalen Bridge at barely walking pace, I realised that I had to get off the coach. Now I just had to convince the driver to open the doors. The coach service was meant to be non-stop all the way to Gloucester Green bus station, but there was no way I could wait that long: it could be another half-hour at least.

We were only a couple of hundred yards from where I needed to be, so I rushed to the front of the coach, hand over my mouth, and yelled at the driver, "Open the doors, I've got to get off, I'm going to be sick."

"I can't let you off here," he replied. "It's against regulations. There's a toilet at the back of the coach: use that."

"There's someone in there," I protested, and leaning closely in towards him and doing my best to look as if I was about to vomit, I added, "Seriously this is an emergency and I'm going to throw up all over you if you don't open these doors."

He relented, pulled a lever, and the doors opened just opposite Rose Lane at the entrance to the botanical gardens.

"Cheers, mate!" I shouted, and leapt off the bus and ran up the High Street as fast as I possibly could. It was 5.03pm. If he was there, I hoped he'd wait. My nineteen-year-old legs covered the ground in no time, and as I reached Magpie Lane on the left, I sprinted across the road and up the short alley that led to the Radcliffe Camera. Exhausted and out of breath, I looked around me, desperately trying to see if I could recognise the face that I'd last seen over 30 years ago.

There had been railings around the large, circular building in the future, but they were gone now, and there were tourists sitting on the steps. A young blonde girl and a boy in a denim jacket were sharing a bottle of wine and laughing in the sunshine. But I could see no one who looked like Josh. What an idiot I was. This was a complete waste of time.

Then a man caught my eye, middle-aged with greying hair and glasses and the beginnings of a pot belly. What was noticeable about him was that he was holding some sort of wand-like device that looked like something out of a science-fiction film. It certainly looked out of place in 1990. He looked like he was looking for someone. Could this be him? He looked so old. I had nothing to lose by approaching him.

"Josh?" I asked tentatively, afraid of looking like an idiot if it turned out to be a case of mistaken identity.

He turned to look at me, and I could see that it was the same man. The face was older, lined with age, but it was unmistakeably him. "Oh my God," he said, "Thomas. You know, I really didn't expect for one minute that you'd actually be here."

"Same here," I said. "I'm so glad you are, though. You wouldn't believe what I've gone through to get here today." And I told him the story about my race against time to get back to Oxford against the odds.

"We need to go somewhere to talk," he said, and we headed back to the High Street and walked down to the Queen's Lane Coffee House.

"I can't get over how young you look," he said. "Last time I saw you, you looked like…well I guess you probably looked a bit like me. How old are you now?"

"I'm nineteen," I said. "I was 51 the last time we met."

"How weird is that?" remarked Josh. "I'm 51 now, and I was nineteen when you met me at Cheltenham Races. I've travelled over 60 years backwards in time to get here today. In 1990, I haven't even been born yet."

"So how long did it take you to work out how to travel back in time?" I asked.

"A very long time," replied Josh, and over coffee he related to me the story of how he'd discovered the existence of Time Bubbles and ultimately how to create his own.

"That's what this little device does," he said, reaching into his pocket and pulling out the wand-like object I had seen earlier. "I can programme this to open a bubble to wherever I want to go to in time. You wouldn't believe the things I've seen. But I guess that can wait until another day. You want to see your future and that's where I am going to take you."

He pulled a second, identical wand out of his pocket. "Only one person can travel within a Bubble at any one time," he explained, "but fortunately I've brought along a spare. I've already preprogrammed both of them. All we need to do is find the right place to create the bubbles, and away we go. I try to avoid doing it in public. It doesn't do to draw attention to people disappearing and appearing in mid-air."

"So where are we going, then?" I asked. "Should we go back to my house in Botley? There won't be anyone there: my parents are in Greece."

"Probably not a good idea," said Josh. "There might not be anyone there now, but what about when we come out of the other end of the Time Bubble? Anyway, I've already got everything planned out. I've already been to your future and I think you'll be pleased with what you'll see. Come on, drink up, we've got a bus to catch."

"Well there's no shortage of them around here," I joked, and Josh laughed. We'd both lived through different eras of time in

Oxford, but there was one constant that never changed: the place was always crammed with buses.

We went to Cornmarket Street, which was now in the days before it was pedestrianised, and jumped on a 2A bus heading north.

"Where are we headed?" I asked.

"I thought you'd have guessed that. We're going to your future home in North Oxford."

I hadn't seen the old place for years, but I'd often thought about it, remembering the happy times I'd had there with Sarah and Stacey. I still missed them terribly even after all this time. Was I going to see them again today?

We got off the bus a couple of stops after we'd passed through Summertown, and walked down the leafy avenue towards the old house. The road still looked exactly the same as I remembered it. Even the trees didn't look any different. They must have been here for decades. There was a certain timeless quality about some parts of Oxford, and this was definitely one of them.

Josh walked straight up to my old house, reached up above the six foot-high gate that led to the secluded and large garden, and undid the bolt on the other side. He'd obviously done this before.

I thought it was a bit odd, marching straight into what was someone else's garden and anticipating my concern, he said, "Don't worry, they're on holiday."

The garden was set to patio at the top, lawn in the middle, and at the far end was a large selection of bushes and fruit trees that Stacey used to call "The Jungle". It hadn't changed much since my time. Josh led me down to this area, right to the bottom where we were out of sight of the main part of the garden.

"This is the best place," he said, "we don't want to be seen." He explained what we were going to do.

He opened his bag and pulled out the two wands, handing one of them to me. "Take hold of this and I'll explain how we are going to travel to the future."

He pressed a red button in the base, illuminating the device. Pressing some further buttons on a small keypad he entered a date and time on a tiny screen built into the top of the device.

*30th July 2035. 4.40pm.*

"Now it's primed," he said. "Hold onto that and don't touch anything." He then did the same with the second device. "Now we are ready to go. All you need to do is copy everything I do."

He held the device out in front of him, and said, "All you need to do now is press the green button and you are ready to go. Like this," and he pressed the button. If I was expecting some spectacular-looking vortex to appear, I was disappointed.

"Nothing happened," I said.

"Oh it did," replied Josh. "You just can't see it." Now, remember what I did, and copy me. He stepped forward two paces and vanished.

I did the same: pressed the green button on my wand, took a deep breath and stepped into the Bubble.

Instantly, I could see the change. The jungle was more overgrown than I'd ever seen it and the light was brighter, with the sun much higher in the sky. Josh was waiting for me.

"Pretty cool, huh?" he said. "It only took me about 30 years to work out how to do it."

I could hear the sound of children laughing and playing from the garden. "Come and take a look," said Josh. "But stay out of sight."

I peered through a gap in the bushes to see an idyllic family scene. I recognised Sarah instantly, older, but still beautiful, with a middle-aged man standing beside her, flipping burgers on a large gas barbecue. After a few seconds, the realisation dawned that it was me. It was 2035, ten years after I'd died, first time round, but I looked fit, tanned and healthy, better than I can ever recall looking in those final years of my life.

Stacey and David were sipping white wine from glasses, chatting away with Sarah and my older self. And two little boys were running around on the lawn, full of energy.

"Are they...?" I began to ask.

"Yes," Josh interrupted. "They are your grandchildren."

"Can we stay a while," I said.

"Of course," said Josh. "Stay as long as you want. Just make sure they don't see you."

I couldn't tear my eyes away. Just being here had answered so many questions. I truly had made a difference. Both Sarah and I were still alive, Stacey was happy with David, and we had two beautiful grandchildren. I'd probably never know why I'd been given the second chance I had, but I had used the time well. My future was secure, my family were happy, and I could go on with my life now without having to worry anymore.

Josh had an extremely futuristic-looking digital camera with him, and took a couple of snaps through the hedge.

"I thought you'd like a memento," he said. "As I figured you wouldn't have been able to bring any pictures back through time with you."

"And I still won't be able to," I said.

"Trust me," he said. "You will."

Reluctant as I was to leave, there was no more I could do here. If I'd walked out onto the lawn and introduced myself, there was no knowing if my future self would have any clue at all about the life I had led. In all likelihood I would be taken for a trespasser, leading to an unpleasant scene. I didn't want to disrupt their day that way.

Josh primed the wands again, and took us back to 1990. Then it was time for him to go back to his own time. But he had one last thing to tell me before he left.

"When you get back home tonight, go into the garage, and find the loose brick underneath your dad's workbench. I've left something there for you." And with that he vanished.

Intrigued, I made my way back to my parents' home in Botley. It was dark by now, but I flicked on the light in the garage, and made my way to the bench at the back as he'd instructed. I reached right underneath, and, true to his word, there was a loose brick there. Underneath, I found a faded white envelope, crinkled and yellowed at the edges with time, with my name written on it.

Inside there was a note attached to the back of a photograph, which read *"Thought you might appreciate this. Best wishes, Josh. 12<sup>th</sup> September 1973."*

I turned over the photograph to see the picture of my family, enjoying that sunny afternoon in the garden, 45 years in the future. At last I had something to remember them by.

# Youth

**August 1987**

I was stretched out on a sunbed next to the swimming pool in a caravan park in the south of France. It was a gloriously hot day, and the sun beat down upon me through an unbroken blue sky. I had my eyes closed and was listening to music on my Walkman.

It played only cassettes. Although CDs were around at this time, they were the preserve only of the rich. My music collection had shrunk over the years and I was making do now with only a handful of pre-bought tapes and numerous blanks upon which I'd recorded music from the radio.

It was one of those tapes that I was listening to now. It seemed that first time round as a teenager I had been in the habit of recording the weekly Top 40 show from the radio on Sunday afternoons. This particular tape, a TDK D120, had been around a while, and the content changed on a weekly basis as I taped over it again and again.

I enjoyed listening to the Top 40. It was a hugely popular show and many of my friends recorded it, too. It was a very common tradition among teenagers at the time, and the only way many could afford to have their own copies of the latest hits. Whether it was legal or not was a bit of a grey area, but as far as I could see it was harmless enough. It certainly wasn't in the same league as all the illegal peer-to-peer file sharing that went on later.

Some of my friends tried to stop the tape at the right moment to cut out the DJ's voice, but I quite enjoyed listening to

Bruno Brookes giving the chart rundown. It was quite a thrill to hear songs that I had known for years now being played at the time they were actually hits. The whole thing had a real retro quality to it.

This was the last one I'd taped before I came away, and it was packed with classic hits, including the Pet Shop Boys who were at number one that week during the height of their fame. I found some of the elements of the show irritating, though. Because it was only two hours long, there wasn't time to play all 40 songs, so they tended to miss out those between positions 21 to 40 that were going down the charts. This included a couple of my favourites that week, one of which had only gone down one measly place to number 31, but wasn't deemed worthy of a play. What I did find rather quaint was the failure to play George Michael's latest single, *I Want Your Sex,* which was in the top ten at the time. In fact, during the countdown, Bruno didn't even refer to it by its full title, referring to it simply as *I Want.*

How times had changed: it seemed that in 1987 you were not even allowed to say the word 'sex' on the radio. As for George Michael's song, it was incredibly tame by the standards of the stuff that had been around a decade or two later. By then it was perfectly acceptable to thrust the likes of a scantily clad Christina Aguilera into every living room in front of impressionable kids of all ages. And as for the lyrics, Eminem and others had pushed the boundaries way beyond what had been acceptable in the 80s. Yet, in other ways, society had moved in the opposite direction. It seemed that it was deemed quite acceptable for football crowds to make monkey noises and throw bananas at black footballers, to which nobody batted an eyelid. It was a strange world, regardless of whether you moved forwards or backwards in time, where values were constantly changing: some for better, others for worse.

The tape ended, and I turned it over and started again, kicking off with Jackie Wilson who had entered the charts at No. 39 with a golden oldie, even by 1986 standards. It seemed there had been a bit of a 50s and 60s revival going on, hence Jackie's return to the charts long after his death. As I listened, I reflected on the past three years.

I had been remarkably relaxed since my trip with Josh to 2035. Now that I knew the future was secure, I could really get on with enjoying the present, and enjoyable years they had certainly been.

Between September 1987 and June 1989, I had been doing my A Levels at the Oxford College of Further Education, referred to locally by all as 'Oxpens'. It was opposite the ice rink, close to the centre of Oxford, and the location of two of the most fun years of my life.

On arriving at the time of completing my A Levels, I swiftly acquired a huge group of friends, hardly any of whom I had seen after I'd left. In this pre-social media age, all I had to keep in touch with people was a small red address book that I'd kept for years, full of names and numbers of people who were unknown to me. Now, at last, I was putting names to those faces.

Life at the college seemed to be one long party and I wondered how I'd ever managed to pass my exams. The college day was split mainly into 90-minute lectures that began at set times. Nearly all of mine seemed to be either from 9.30am until 11.00am or from 3.00pm to 4.30pm. This meant that I had a four-hour gap in the middle which coincided precisely with the opening hours of The

Duke of York, a public house conveniently situated just across from the entrance to the college.

It seemed that the entire daytime social life of the college revolved around this pub, where a half of lager at 53p a pop could be made to last a good hour or so for your average poor student. I was still pretty well off thanks to the bookies, but it was getting increasingly difficult to get bets on as I continued to get younger. The pub itself tended to turn a blind eye to the underage drinking going on, which was hardly surprising. It was doing a roaring trade at lunchtimes thanks to the college, and takings would have been severely dented if they'd started asking for ID. Unfortunately the bookies were a lot stricter, and even at the age of 21 I was finding myself being frequently asked for ID, usually when I was collecting rather than putting bets on, which was typical. They were happy to take stake money from underage gamblers. But if they then had the audacity to win, the bookie would ask for ID and, if the punter could not provide it, would confiscate the cash.

Once my eighteenth birthday came and went in October 1988, I was in real difficulty. Any sizeable win, and my age was immediately brought into question. I didn't possess any sort of fake ID, and had neither the means nor the time to create one on a daily basis with the limited resources at my disposal. Reluctantly, other than getting in my dad's good books by tipping him a few winners for his Saturday Lucky 15 bet, I had to concede that my gambling days were over.

There was still a lot of fun to be had in the pub and I don't think I ever enjoyed myself quite as much as during those two years. Darts, bar billiards and an ancient old console game called Pac-Man were all part of the fun. There was also a long-standing tradition where we all dutifully trooped into the poolroom to watch the lunchtime showing of *Neighbours* on an old-fashioned cathode ray TV attached to the wall. It seemed the whole college stopped one memorable November day in 1988, when the pub was packed to the rafters with students ready to witness Scott and Charlene's wedding.

The two years at college flew by. Disappointingly, it had been a pretty lean spell for girlfriends, though I had managed to have a few brief liaisons with girls from college. Suddenly, it was the beginning of September, and other than one lad who had come to the college with me from school, my newfound friends vanished as swiftly as they'd arrived.

I still had Simone to look forward to and I got a thrill each time a new letter from her popped through the door, even though I'd read them all dozens of times before. They were coming in thick and fast throughout August. I never replied to any of them, my predecessor had already done that for me, so there seemed little point. Now, lying beside the pool, I knew that I was one day away from seeing her.

Like when I'd met Sarah in Ibiza, our holidays had not exactly aligned, and I knew that Simone had left the park before I had. My holiday had ended on the 11th of August, but she had left on the 6th. I knew she was going to be in the next caravan to us, so on that morning I was out of bed the second I awoke, pulling aside the curtains on the static caravan, to try and get a glimpse of her next door. Sure enough, there she was, wearing the orange blouse and black skirt that she had in one of the pictures I'd kept of her. Her parents were in an advanced state of loading up their car to go home, so I dressed quickly and hurried outside to see her.

They were nearly ready to leave, so she excused herself from her parents to take a quick walk with me around the site. Her father seemed none too happy about it and was pretty grumpy when she said she'd be back soon, telling her to "dépêche-toi".

We walked hand-in-hand up towards the entertainment block by the pool, where she pulled me to her and kissed me deeply. There were tears in her eyes as she repeated "Je t'aime" over and over again. We had time only for the briefest of goodbyes before we reluctantly parted, she promising in her broken English to write as soon as she got home.

It wasn't difficult to see why I'd been attracted to her. She was fiery and passionate, and I found her French accent incredibly sexy. I must have had a thing about accents, because it had been just the same with Sarah and many others. As for the sex with Simone, it was some of the best I'd ever had. It went on for several days, all over the site, in the showers reserved for the campers, on the beach at night, wherever and whenever the opportunity arose.

The first time it happened was in my caravan, when my parents had gone out on a wine-tasting trip to a local vineyard. I knew they would get drunk and not be back for hours. It was only the third day of my holiday, but we were already an item by this time. She was all over me as soon as she joined me at the pool that morning, as I soaked up yet another day of sunshine.

When she began kissing me passionately on the sunbed, getting extremely heated, I knew what she wanted. And no one could have wanted it more than me. This was a pivotal moment in a young man's life. I was about to lose my virginity. It wasn't going to be quite the cause for celebration for me that it was for every other male on the planet, though: quite the opposite in fact. I was going to have to savour this because it was going to be the last shag I'd ever have.

I wondered to myself how many people living a normal life knew when they were having their last shag? Not many, I reckoned, and even if they did and were very old at the time, the likelihood was that their sex drive would have waned and they wouldn't be that bothered anyway. In my case, I had to face years of rampant teenage hormones with nothing to look forward to at the end of it. It was a depressing thought, but I wasn't going to let it spoil the moment. That last afternoon in my tiny single bed in the caravan was one of the most memorable of my entire life. I couldn't really complain. From Marie to Simone, and all the others in-between, I'd had more than my fair share of sexual adventures, as well as an extremely fulfilling marriage. I'd truly had the best of both worlds.

**December 1984**

I didn't give up trying to have sex with more girls in the years that followed. After all, perhaps, I'd be able to use my unique knowledge to my advantage in the same way that I had with Carol. But sadly the only thing I managed to pull in my early teenage years was myself. Once I reached my fifteenth birthday, I knew the game was up. Contrary to what some of the boastful idiots in my class said, girls just weren't ready to go "all the way" at that age. At least not the ones I knew anyway, and my choice was limited. I had been at an all boys' school between the ages of eleven and sixteen which hadn't helped, and the girls at the church youth club certainly weren't willing to indulge me. I managed a few snogs at parties and the odd hand inside a bra here and there, but that was about as far as it went. It was incredibly frustrating and depressing. At least the average teenage boy, wanking two or three times a day, had the realistic hope that sooner or later they would manage to get a girl to have sex with them. I didn't even have that consolation.

So, by December 1984, I had resigned myself to a life of celibacy. Sex wasn't the only avenue of pleasure that was becoming closed off to me. Gambling had long gone, and I also had to adjust to a life without alcohol. Even The Duke wouldn't serve kids as young as me. A brief dalliance with the Kidlington Young Farmers provided a couple of drunken nights at barn dances on dubious home-made cider from the farm, but teetotalism was looming large.

Perhaps it was just as well, because my tolerance to alcohol was fast disappearing. A week before Christmas 1984, I'd attended a house party of one of my school friends. There had been some illicit alcohol on the go, out of the sight of parents. I only drank about three cans of cider, but that was more than enough to get me legless and lead to me chucking up all over the kitchen floor when I got home. My mum was not happy and nor was I. For someone who'd once been effortlessly able to knock back ten pints on a Friday night, this was a poor show indeed.

My best friend at the time was a lad from school called Martin who was obsessed with playing computer games. It seemed that we spent most Sundays together during the winter playing on our ZX Spectrums, incredibly primitive machines compared to those in the future. They were hugely popular at the time, though, and even I had to admit that they did provide a fair bit of entertainment considering their limitations. Martin's favourite was a game called

Football Manager, which actually wasn't too bad, though I found it very hard to suppress my giggles at the little stickman graphics.

The programmers achieved quite a lot with a machine with 48k of RAM, a tiny fraction of the capacity of the computers of the 21st century. *Jet Set Willy*, *Sabre Wulf* and *Knight Lore* were among some of the biggest games of 1984, and if you could get over the simple block graphics and horrible colour clashes they were quite addictive. Most games were controlled by the keyboard, but I did have something called a Kempston joystick as well. I attempted to use this several times, but it appeared to be broken. Eventually one day it started working which was the day I discovered how it had got broken – with some rather overenthusiastic waggling during the 100 metres whilst playing *Daley Thompson's Decathlon*.

The most frustrating thing about this computer was that I had to load in the games using a small tape recorder. It took several minutes and frequently the computer would crash at the end of the loading process. This tape recorder doubled as my only way of playing recorded music, the Walkman now long gone. I used to listen to my top 40 tapes in the evening until John Peel came on to Radio 1 which I listened to on a tiny handheld AM radio. Peel used to have indie bands in to the studio to do sessions, and I looked forward to those late nights listening to sessions from such greats as Depeche Mode and The Smiths on 275 metres medium wave.

I was becoming aware of my own mortality. Although everyone had to face the fact that they were going to die at some point, most were spared knowing exactly when. But I knew that I had just fourteen years left. In reality, it would be less than that, as I wasn't going to be able to do a lot in the first couple of years, remembering Stacey as a baby. What would it be like? Would I remember any of my future life at all? Would I care about anything other than getting fed and having my nappy changed? Grown-ups couldn't remember being babies, so was I destined to suffer the same fate in reverse?

As I huddled under the covers, on those cold winter evenings in late-1984, I began to feel very alone and very afraid.

**June 1982**

It was my final term at primary school and I was adjusting to my new environment. The place was full of little kids and I had to come to terms with the fact that I would soon be one of them. My memories of my adult life remained with me and at times I felt old beyond my years, but I just did my best to adapt as I went along.

Changes were happening to me, both mentally and physically. I'd been through puberty in reverse and now it was over, I had reappraised my situation with regard to girls. Having to give up sex wasn't really any big deal anymore. In fact, I found the whole idea quite distasteful. As for girls, far from finding them attractive, I now just considered them an annoyance. Given a choice between playing football with my mates and hanging out with a girl, my mates won every time.

Even using Martin's telescope to spy on the woman who lived opposite him when she got out of the shower didn't excite me anymore. The whole subject of sex just seemed silly and embarrassing to me now. As for self-pleasuring, I'd packed that in a long time ago, sometime around my 13th birthday. I spent most of my free time now hanging out with friends, either out and about, or on my computer which had now been downgraded to a ZX81. This made the Spectrum look like rocket science, but there wasn't that much else to do.

Board games were pretty popular, and I was pleased that a lot of the games that I'd played as an adult were still around. I loved a good game of Monopoly, and my clever strategy of building just three houses on each property was normally good enough to outwit my friends.

Football stickers, matchbox cars, marbles and more – all of these things that had once seemed childish to me were beginning to seem like good fun. The adult world I had once lived in seemed distant, and may as well have been on another planet for all the relevance it had to me now. Occasionally I would go down to the garage, pull out the brick and take a look at the picture of my future family, but the more I looked at it, the more they looked like strangers. I loved my mum and dad; they were my family now, not to mention my grandparents, all of whom had entered my life during the 1980s.

The last time I looked at the photo was one Sunday afternoon in June, when I'd been helping my dad in the garden. I'd gone into the garage to put the lawnmower away. We'd had the radio on in the garden for the Top 40, and I could hear Tommy Vance counting down the chart towards the No. 1, which that week was *House of Fun* by Madness.

I took out the photo and looked at the faces I would never see again. They meant so little to me now. I put the photo back behind the brick, and went off down to the park to play cricket with my mates until it got dark.

**May 1974**

I went to play school on two days a week, and on the other three I went to Grampy and Granny's house, a place full of excitement and adventure for a three-year-old boy.

On Mondays, Granny used to do her washing using an old-fashioned mangle. I loved watching her squeeze the clothes through the rollers. At lunchtime, she would cook me some fish fingers and chips. She used to cook the chips using a big white block of lard she'd melt in a pan. They were delicious, much nicer than the ones my mum and dad made. I would sit at the round table in their living room to eat them and Granny would put the telly on so I could watch *Rainbow*. My favourite was Zippy, he was really funny and I loved it when he was naughty and got his mouth stitched up.

After lunch, I would go with Grampy into the back garden to feed the chickens. There were four of them and I had given them all names. He said we were going to eat one of them for Sunday dinner, but I think he was just joking.

In the afternoon Grampy liked to go and get his paper from the shop at the bottom of the street and he always took me with him and gave me 6p to spend on sweets. I would point at one of the jars on the shelf and the nice lady behind the till would weigh a few into a little white paper bag for me.

I was a little confused about how life worked. I heard my parents and other people talk about growing up, but it didn't seem to make sense to me. Sometimes my parents started sentences with phrases like "When you were a baby, you used to..." but I didn't have any memory of being a baby. I thought I used to be bigger. Sometimes at night I'd have strange dreams about people that seemed vaguely familiar to me, and faraway places I couldn't remember ever seeing. It all made very little sense to my three-year-old brain.

Some of the things that my parents said confused me. They would say things like "We're going on holiday tomorrow, are you looking forward to it?" when it would seem to me that we had just come back. Perhaps they were getting their words mixed up. When they said tomorrow, they must have meant yesterday. Or maybe it was me. I was still learning words and I got them wrong sometimes. I was sure I'd figure it all out eventually.

# Birth

**21st October 1970**

It was warm inside, dark, wet and comforting. I hadn't been here before, but I liked it. I tried to breathe but I couldn't. It seemed like I didn't need to, though. I was aware that there was some sort of tube attached to my stomach, but I had no idea what it was for.

There wasn't much room to move about, and before long, I started to feel a great weight pushing me forwards. There were contractions all around me, forcing me into a tight tube, head downwards. I didn't know where I was going but I didn't like it and tried to fight against it.

Suddenly, there was a bright light, forcing my eyes shut against the glare. I was outside, in a world full of light and noise. I involuntarily cried and gasped for breath. There were people around me and I could hear voices. How I knew that, I didn't know, but I knew I had been here before.

I didn't know the meaning of the words the people spoke. Had I been able to, I would have heard a nurse say: "Congratulations, Mrs Scott. It's a boy."

And then I was in the comforting arms of my mother, recognising her immediately. I definitely had been here before. I looked greedily at her nipples, my own personal milk machine, and couldn't wait to suck on them.

The rest of the day was a blur of feeding, sleeping and having my nappy changed, much like any other day. I didn't really have any concept of time, but my instincts suggested I'd be back inside the warm, wet place soon.

I was wrong.

**22nd October 1970**

It was morning. I was in my cot, next to my mother's hospital bed, when my father came in. Something didn't seem right, but it wasn't something that my immature brain was able to work out. I watched as my father moved over to my mother's bedside table, and listened to the conversation. The words made little sense to me, but the voices were familiar and comforting.

Something told me I shouldn't be here. I should be snug in the warm, wet confines of my mother's womb. That was the way things were supposed to work.

I couldn't read. If I had been able to I would have noticed the sticker on the side of my cot that read "Thomas Scott, born 21st Oct 1970". I couldn't read the calendar on the bedside table either. It was one of those little square ones with a page for every day of the year that you tore off.

"You didn't change the calendar," said my father, as he tore the page reading "21 Oct", leaving "22 Oct" exposed.

None of this meant anything to me. If it had, I would have realised for the first time in over 54 years that time was moving forward for me once again. I wasn't destined to shrink inside my mother's womb until all that was left was an egg and a sperm. The moment of my birth had restarted the clock.

"He's amazing," said my mother, "and he's got his whole life in front of him."

"I wonder what he will be like," said my father. "Just think, when he's grown up it will be nearly the 21st century. He'll see amazing things in the future, things we can't even imagine."

None of this meant anything to my newborn ears. I was tired, and wanted to go back to sleep. I had a long life in front of me.


The End.




If you have enjoyed this story, I'd be hugely grateful if you could help other readers to discover it by leaving a review at amazon.co.uk or amazon.com.

Many thanks

Jason

# Also by Jason Ayres:

# The Time Bubble

Charlie and Josh's interests were the same as most other teenagers: drinking, parties and girls. That was until the day they discovered the Time Bubble.

It starts at a bit of fun, jumping a few seconds into the future. Soon things take a more serious turn as the leaps in time increase in duration. When a teenage girl goes missing, and the police become involved, suspicion falls on Charlie. How can he explain where she is? Will anyone believe him?

As the long term dangers of the Bubble become clear, one man comes up with a solution – one that could hold the key to his own salvation.

Set in a small market town in Southern England in the early 21st century, this light-hearted time travel novel has plenty to delight readers of all ages.

# Also by Jason Ayres:

# Global Cooling

Ten years have passed since Charlie and Josh discovered The Time Bubble. As they wait for Peter to emerge after several years inside, Earth is facing a global climate catastrophe.

The astronomers had predicted that the asteroid would miss our planet. They were wrong. It slams into the Sahara Desert, annihilating everything within a hundred miles. But this is only the beginning. A huge amount of dust is thrown up into the atmosphere, blocking out the sun across the planet. Soon temperatures begin to fall.

As weather conditions worsen, the members of The Time Bubble team need to make a decision – flee south to escape the weather, or wait for the worst to pass. Choosing to stay, D.I. Hannah Benson soon has more to worry about than keeping law and order. With power supplies failing and food scarce, it soon becomes a battle just to stay alive. And there are some that see it not as a crisis, but as an opportunity.

Set a decade after the main events of The Time Bubble, this sequel takes place in parallel with events in the latter stages of that story.

# About the author

Jason Ayres began his writing career at Primary School in 1979 with a 94 chapter epic space adventure. It featured the exploits of Captain Jason who bore more than a passing resemblance to a famous starship captain of the era. Sadly, the plot was just getting going when his teacher firmly suggested that he try writing about something else.

Never one to let the creative sap rest for long, by the mid 1980's he was furiously scribbling down plays in "spare" exercise books liberated from the stationery cupboard. These plays starred his classmates and girls he fancied in a number of outrageous and libellous scenarios. The plays have now been placed securely under lock and key with strict instructions never to release them to the general public.

Unfortunately his budding aspirations as a writer were somewhat stifled in his twenties by an ill-advised fifteen year career in the Market Research industry. At this time, writing opportunities were somewhat limited by having to go to work every day. However he still found time to write numerous letters to various manufacturers advising them on their product ranges. He also produced many spoof newsletters for the countless activities that a social life based around the pub entailed.

Eventually he left the world of sales figures behind to become a stay-at-home dad, giving him a whole new source of material to write about. His first two humorous parenting diaries, "Fortysomething Father" and "Austerity Dad", were published in 2013. This was followed in 2014 by a third diary recording his experiences in the world of sausages. He also continued writing about his parenting experiences via a weekly column in the Oxford Mail.

In the summer of 2014 Jason released his first novel, "The Time Bubble", which was a huge hit both in the UK and the US, achieving the coveted #1 spot in the YA Time Travel category. The sequel, "Global Cooling" followed in November.

In March 2015, he released his latest time travel epic, "My Tomorrow, Your Yesterday". This story of a man living his life backwards, one day at a time, is set in Oxford between the years 2025 and 1970, and is ideal material for a film, according to the author!

Want to know more about Jason? - find him on Twitter @AusterityDad

Printed in Great Britain
by Amazon